FICTIONS
OF AN
IMMIGRANT

Roberto Porta-Córdoba

ISBN: 978-0-578-84059-8 (Paperback)

Library of Congress Control Number: 2021901151

Portions of this book are works of fiction. Any references to historical events, real people, or real places are used fictitiously. Other names, characters, places and events are products of the author's imagination, and any resemblances to actual events or places or persons, living or dead, is entirely coincidental.

Portions of this book are works of nonfiction. Certain names and identifying characteristics have been changed.

Front cover image by Rogier Hoekstra,
https://pixabay.com/photos/dreams-fantasy-art-surreal-2904682/

Book design by Roberto Porta Córdoba

Printed in the United States of America.

First printing edition 2021.

Ingram Content Group
1 Ingram Blvd,
La Vergne, TN 37086

roberto.porta@comcast.net

Dedication

To my patient and ever supporting wife,
to my ingenious four sons, and
to all the selfless teachers of the world,
        -this book is sincerely dedicated to you.

"There is no greater agony than bearing an untold story inside you."

Maya Angelou

Table of Contents

Roberto Porta-Córdoba

In the Swirl of Power

Alicia was a girl of humble extraction. Thanks to her outstanding grades, she had obtained a scholarship at one of the top universities in the country and pursued a career in international relations. After 18 months of grueling internship, she had been hired as a protocol specialist at the Ministry of Foreign Affairs. It was there where she met Honorato Melgar. It was there where Honorato broke her heart.

Honorato, a man in his mid-thirties, occupied a highly coveted position in government, as the president's personal aide. His position was not intellectually challenging, neither was he considered an advisor or a counselor. He was rather a glorified gofer, what presidents call a "body man", the man with the Sharpie, the man who makes sure the water bottle is always full. Nevertheless, he followed the president wherever he went, helping him stick to his agenda, and serving as the visible pivot of all ceremonial and official events. All things considered, he was important. He was in the swirl of power.

Alicia fell for Honorato's looks and verbosity after several work-related encounters. One of the paradoxical perks of presiding over one of the poorest countries in Latin America was the large influx of foreign aid the nation could receive. The president spent a lot of time thanking the foreign generosity at the frequent ceremonials held at the Ministry of Foreign Affairs. Alicia got to see Honorato at least once a week. His elegance, his politeness, the funny notes he wrote to her, and the small presents he

1

surprised her with, made Alicia fell for him. A romantic relation ensued.

Sadly, the romance didn't last long. Because of Honorato's hectic work schedule -which mirrored the president's- they barely had private time for each other. After three months, Alicia realized that she knew more about Honorato's cologne and shirt preferences than about his personal life or goals. Their complex work schedule limited their time together to improvised and vertiginous dates of almost furtive nature. Honorato would call her unexpectedly to whisper a place and time to meet, sometimes at the oddest hours and at the remotest places. She always complied without a gripe. She admired him. She was in love.

The rude awakening was inevitable. Such is the fate of living in a fairytale or simply the fate of living in a small town. One night, as she was exiting a grocery store, Alicia caught eye of Honorato. He drove into the parking lot with a woman in the passenger seat. Unaware he was being watched, he got off the car and walked to the entrance with his arm around the woman's shoulder and a little girl holding his other hand. Alicia cried silently all the way home, hiding her tears from the taxi driver and wondering how she could have been so stupid.

When confronted, Honorato clumsily tried to justify himself by admitting that he was married but "considering separation" and that he didn't think "it was important" to inform Alicia about his personal troubles "for the time being." Alicia gave Honorato the cold shoulder and stopped talking to him altogether, shifting non-essential communication with the

2

president's protocol office to another colleague. She was hurt. Honorato tried to make things up several times, but gave up after several weeks when he realized he had burned the bridges and Alicia wanted nothing to do with him.

For a while, things seemed normal at the office. Alicia was a discreet woman and didn't share much of her personal life with anyone at work. Also, she had never been a resentful person or the kind that held a grudge for too long. She didn't dwell in the past. Born in poverty and dealing with constant challenges, she had learned since a young age to be practical and let bygones be bygones. Honorato's deceit would've been forgotten if it wasn't because –probably with his ego still bruised- he said something in a work meeting about Alicia's social status that went beyond the boundaries of what she considered an acceptable joke. Oblivious to the underlying tension, everyone laughed and celebrated the pun, but Alicia felt that Honorato had crossed the line. Alicia felt insulted.

It is here where American writer Edgar Allan Poe comes into the story. Alicia had been an avid reader since childhood, maybe because used books were some of the few "toys" her parents could afford. Days after Honorato's disrespect, she came across "The Cask of Amontillado", Poe's short story in which a man takes revenge on another by burying him alive. In the story, a character named Montresor narrates how he had to put up with "the thousand injuries" from his friend Fortunato, but he adds that when Fortunato "ventured upon insult", he had "vowed revenge."

Of course, Alicia had no intention of killing anybody, let alone burying him alive, but for the first

3

time in her 25 years, she felt the desire to revolt, to get back at adversity, to settle the score with the imbalances of life, to retaliate at humiliation. She kept on reading Poe's story. When she finished it near midnight, she stayed thoughtful for a few minutes, she looked at her monthly agenda… and vowed revenge.

In the story, Montresor says that an avenger "must not only punish, but punish with impunity." Alicia knew that she had to act with the greatest care. She could not suffer because of taking her revenge. While she put her plan together, she gave no clue to Honorato or anybody about her discomfort. She continued fulfilling her protocol duties, supporting the president's staff as needed, coordinating trips abroad, overseeing documents, and handling all the worldly affairs of diplomacy. However, she started looking for a job somewhere else.

The chance for retribution came soon. The president had to travel to Morocco in three weeks. The young leader of that Northern African nation, King Mohammed VI, only 37 at the time, needed all the political support he could get in his diplomatic struggle for Western Sahara, a territory in historical dispute with the Polisario Front. The president's advisors knew an opportunity when they saw one and correctly figured out that a visit of support to the King could bring much-needed commercial trade for the country and enhanced the image of the president at home for his upcoming reelection bid.

In Poe's story, Montresor also says that to achieve true revenge it's not enough that an offender pays for his faults. He claims that true revenge occurs when the offender knows *who* is making him pay for

4

them. Following this premise, Alicia sent an e-mail to Honorato informing him about Morocco's culture and suggesting some items to be used in the official gift exchange between the two leaders. She recommended that the president presented Mohammed VI with a miniature handmade ship -fishermen and sails included- made of national precious wood. That would celebrate the famous skill and tradition of Morocco's fishermen and at the same time exhibit the beautiful work of the nation's handcrafters whom the president represented. To supplement the gifts, she also suggested presenting the monarch with a frozen sample of the finest local pelibuey meat –a breed of domestic sheep raised in the tropic- to promote its exportation. Although surprised by the e-mail and the suggestions, Honorato thought they were both great ideas and thanked Alicia. He told the president and took credit for the ideas, receiving many compliments from the presidential team for his "consistent wit and dedication."

By the time the president's trip neared, Alicia had already accepted a new position at a non-governmental organization and had given her two-week notice at the Ministry of Foreign Affairs. Helping Honorato with all the details of the Morocco trip would be her last job. This trip meant a lot to the president. It was a strategic move and he demanded his staff to treat it with the highest priority and attention to detail. His image at home depended on the political gains of the visit, and those gains depended on impression he would make on the King. Honorato worked long hours with the Ministry of Foreign Affairs polishing the agenda, checking the quality of the official presents, and comprising the trip's dossier for the president.

On a sunny morning of July, the president and his entourage met the King of one of the fastest changing Islamic countries of the world. Dozens of local reporters were in attendance, curious to meet the statesman from a small country in Central America who had crossed the Atlantic to offer his political support. Trained by Honorato, the president greeted Mohammed VI in Arabic, which pleased the affable but serious monarch. After the formal introductions and questions from the press, it was time for the customary gift exchange. As the host, the King went first, presenting the president with a beautifully crafted tall vase representative of Moroccan ceramic, followed by a traditional hand-woven rug. The sound of the clicking cameras flooded the hall while the president thanked the King and posed with the huge vase and the rug before passing them to Honorato behind him.

It was then the president's turn. With a smile on his face and a gesture of his head, he signaled Honorato to bring his presents to the King. He brought a large pack nicely wrapped in colorful bright paper. The president proudly presented it to the monarch, explaining to him that it was a large frozen sample of the best tropical sheep meat produced in his country. Mohammed VI thanked him and proceeded to remove the paper wrap. The cameras clicked again, but the King looked puzzled. The vacuum sealed bag was labeled "bacon" in big letters. The reporters laughed. The president smiled nervously while Honorato's jaw dropped. The King hastily handed the pack to an aide.

The president announced that he had another present and looked at Honorato with cold eyes. He brought in a medium sized box which the president solemnly presented to the King without saying a word. The clicking sound of the cameras was louder this time. Mohammed VI removed the fancy cellophane wrapper and opened the box, but he looked utterly confused. A mumbling from the crowd followed. The King looked inside the box and then to the president, as if not understanding what the gift was. The president smiled timidly, approached the King, and peeked into the box, ready to describe the craft involved in the making of the precious wood ship to the monarch. But there was no ship inside. What they were looking at were several pieces of wood cramped together in bubble wrap and fastened with rubber bands. No one had assembled the ship. The mumbling in the hall turned to giggling and laughter. The president felt a sharp twinge in the stomach. He was mortified. The King thanked the president and graciously pulled him away for a tour of the royal palace. Before turning a corner, the president looked for Honorato amid the crowd of security detail, diplomats, and reporters. When their eyes met, the president gave him the most hateful look a human can give another human.

Honorato was relieved of his duties that same night and sent home the next morning in a commercial flight. When he landed, he was denied the protocol services at the airport; no one from the president's office was waiting for him; his driver didn't answer his calls and neither did his staff at the office. He had to wait for his stunned wife to pick him up. She informed

7

him that the official vehicle assigned to him had been requisitioned that same afternoon; that the toiletry bag he kept at work had been dropped at their home; and that human resources had called requiring his office keys by the following morning.

Honorato's career in government was effectively over, just like his chances of ever landing a formal job again. In small countries like his, employment agencies and hiring managers stayed away from disgraced professionals like him. Honorato spent years applying for jobs and scattering résumés all over town. For half a decade now, no human hand has touched them. May he rest in peace!

Roberto Porta-Córdoba

False Advertising

A fulltime job, finally. After ten months of internship, endless workshops, and lame chores at the newspaper, I would have my own cubicle, my own desk, and my own laptop. No more rookie jokes, no more coffee errands, and no burning midnight oil for others. From now on, I would do it for me. I went out to celebrate with Elvira. We drank more than six martinis each. We ended up nauseous, with jelly legs, and a pounding headache.

Did you know that James Bond has it all wrong when he orders his martinis "shaken, not stirred"? Martinis are meant to be stirred! When you shake a martini, you're making it very cold, very fast. You end up with a very cold drink which feels lighter and almost effervescent. On the other hand, when you stir a martini, you keep the texture of the spirit undisturbed. The drink feels velvety and heavier, the way it's supposcd to be.

And so, with a hangover and all, I showed up for work the following morning. What a thrill! I felt so proud and accomplished. We met with the city editor midmorning. She was picky and meticulous, always reminding reporters about the leads, the nutshell paragraphs, the inverted pyramid structure, and so on. I didn't care. I was elated. My peers congratulated me. They seem genuinely happy for me. Everyone patted me on the back.

9

At the beginning, I dedicated a good part of my shift to help interns, those idealists who, like me, think that journalism is the best career in the world. I still think so, although the anxiety and the swollen feet of the long days can get to me, sometimes. I helped a young girl draw up her first text. Total fail. The poor thing couldn't even type out of nervousness and when she tried to playback an interview she had saved on her old handheld recorder, she ended up deleting it by accident. Unrecoverable. Wasted time.

It would be until my third day on the job that I officially debuted as reporter. I was assigned to cover a lawsuit that a man was filing at the circuit court. My colleague Sergei was headed in that direction on his way to cover a press conference by the governor. I asked him for a lift. I wasn't accredited yet to cover that sort of events. The rookies began with the basic, with the pedestrian.

I didn't know much about the lawsuit, only that the plaint was against a well-known brand and that the plaintiff was backed up by the Bureau of Consumer Protection and two other consumer defense organizations. The fact that the brand was distributed nationwide by a corporation accused of mistreating its employees added fuel to the flames.

When my colleague dropped me off near the courthouse, it surprised me to see a crowd of reporters waiting on the parking lot. I counted at least eight cameramen and around thirty reporters from all kind of media outlets. A few of them knew me from my internship errands and congratulated me for my

10

appointment, the others must have taken me for a freelancer.

A few minutes later, the plaintiff arrived in his lawyer's car. He was welcomed by several activists from one of the consumer defense groups. The man was short and pudgy, with a receding hairline that announced an early baldness, and a pencil thin mustache. He wore an undersized blue jacket and a real tight white shirt that stretched the front buttons. The pants were of a different tone of blue from the jacket and short enough to let his white socks show. The green tie with an amoeba pattern, barely above his belly button, was so wide and short that it almost looked like a bib. The man was sweating profusely in the heat of the early afternoon.

-Who is the defendant? –started one colleague, stretching his mic toward him.

-The lawsuit is against the "Handsome" brand – replied his lawyer instead.

We all knew that "Handsome" was a manufacturer of deodorants and male fragrances with massive advertising campaigns around the world. It was a staple sponsor during broadcasted sports events and its ads were also visible on billboards around the country. The brand invested a fortune on its creative ads in magazines, TV, and social media, in which women are irresistibly swayed by the "Handsome effect, the manly scent of the good looking". The company also manufactured products like styling hair gel, shaving cream, suntan oil, and men's cologne.

-Can you tell us the motives for the lawsuit? – asked another reporter.

11

-My client will gladly share them with you – said the lawyer, making room on the sidewalk for the man.

-The "Handsome" company has lied –said the plaintiff-. I feel scammed.

-How so? –asked a radio reporter.

-The "Handsome" company has lied and has affected me –replied the man.

-But, that is a very famous international company –added another reporter-. How exactly did it lie to you?

The man looked uncomfortable and nervous. His humbleness betrayed him.

-The "Handsome" company didn't keep its promises – he said, in a hesitant voice.

The reporters asked him for his name, age, and where he lived. The man answered with naivety. He said that he was 37 and lived in the suburbs. A real crowd had slowly gathered near the court's entrance. The security guards had to ask the journalists not to block the access.

-How exactly did the company fail to keep its promises? –asked a colleague.

The man looked uncomfortable. He continued to sweat and it was evident that he had used up all the answers rehearsed with his lawyer on the way to the court. He timidly attempted to break through the human wall, but the reporters didn't move an inch. All cameras were on him and their clicks were clearly audible. He had about twenty phones and recorders pointed at his face.

-Thank you, we need to move on –tried to interrupt his lawyer.

12

-Let him tell us how "Handsome" didn't keep its promises –demanded the reporters.

-How is he going to prove that the company lied to him? What does he mean the company lied? Why does he feel scammed? –asked other colleagues.

The man flashed a nervous smile for a millisecond and glanced at his lawyer. The man looked stressed. The lawyer and the activists tried to move him forward.

-Excuse us fellows, excuse us –said the attorney in a frugal tone of voice.

-Can't your client answer these questions? – inquired a female reporter.

-"Handsome" is a prestigious company, but your client doesn't bring any evidence? –inquired another reporter.

The man raised an arm and asked for silence. His armpits were wet. He tried to smile but couldn't.

-Let me explain –he said with difficulty.

The reporters supported his request for silence. It was until then that I activated the voice recorder in my smartphone and got as close as I could to the man, but he didn't say anything. He turned to his lawyer and whispered something in his ear. We all waited.

-My client prefers that I describe the lawsuit against "Handsome" –the lawyer said while putting a hand on the man's shoulder.

Clearing his throat, the attorney slowly said that his client was seeking compensation in the amount of $800,000 for infliction of emotional distress.

-This gentleman has been irresponsibly scammed by a greedy and wicked company through the deliberate practice of false advertising –he said-.

13

My client believed the company's promise that if he used "Handsome" products he would have more probabilities of attracting a woman. He has spent the last three years consuming deodorants, lotions, creams, scents, and other products from that company's catalog without success. Where is the "Handsome" effect, then?

All cameras focused on the man who now showed the reporters some of the deodorants and products with the "Handsome" brand. Some giggles were audible in the crowd. I felt a lump in my throat. The thrill of my first formal assignment was disappearing. Suddenly, I craved for a martini.

-My client fully trusted this debauched, depraved, and devious company –added the attorney in an angry tone while clenching his fist-. Ever since he had access to the corporate world in which he deservingly climbed after years of schooling, dedication, and hard work, my client has tried to establish a formal, serious, and tender relationship with a lady. Incomprehensibly, no lady has accepted him despite smelling his fragrance, despite feeling his scent. Isn't that false advertising? Aren't the "Handsome" ads all about women chasing the man who uses their product? In my client's case, they haven't worked. Rather, they have affected him… they have hurt him… they have scarred him, emotionally and psychologically. This is ludicrous! This is preposterous! This is nefarious!

The plaintiff must have felt redeemed by these words. Like Moses parting the waters at the Red Sea, the man in the tight suit parted the wall of reporters in

14

front of him and managed to walk to the courthouse entrance. His shirt and tie were soaked in transpiration.

-We invite you all to support us in this crusade for the consumer rights, for their protection, for their dignity, for their healing –said the lawyer in a loud voice-. Thank you very much!

Some reporters had a smirk on their faces. Others giggled openly and shook their head. We all turned off our recording devices and some darted to their vehicles ahead of the governor's conference. Only three colleagues, probably interns or freelancers, followed the plaintiff and his lawyer inside the courthouse. I phoned Sergei. Maybe we could have some martinis. This time, shaken, not stirred.

Roberto Porta-Córdoba

The South Florida Incident

Back in the early 90s, I worked as a personnel manager for a large retail store in South Florida. Part of my functions included screening the job applications received in the store every week and selecting the most qualified candidates for a first interview with me. After meeting with them, I picked those that I considered most fitting for each vacancy and set an appointment for a second interview with the corresponding area manager. The ones who I didn't pick went to a waiting list file. Sometimes, my criteria didn't match the one from the area managers and they would ask me for a second option, which I would retrieve from the waiting list file.

Other than the Christmas season, I would normally interview an average of eight applicants every week. Sometimes I had many applications to screen, sometimes I had just a few. There were no online recruiting services back then.

I remember when that applicant walked into my office for his first interview. A mulatto, with lively eyes and frizzly hair. He quickly informed me he was a Cuban rafter. I had already met several Cubans who risked their lives in those dangerous makeshift boats, so I didn't find his story wild or exaggerated.

We conducted the interview in Spanglish and I was impressed with his eloquence and smartness. When we finished, he shook my hand vigorously, and without letting go, he looked at me straight in the eye and begged me to help him get the job. His situation was precarious. He had arrived four months before and

17

had made some poor financial decisions. I don't recall if he mentioned kids or family, but I do remember how overwhelmed he sounded and looked. I explained our hiring process to him. I said that if he didn't hear from us in a couple of days, it meant that we didn't have an opening for him at that time and he would need to wait. When he let go of the handshake and left, I stood there convinced of his sincerity.

That interview happened on a Tuesday morning. My job responsibilities demanded objectivity –and although I wanted to help the Cuban rafter- I realized there were more qualified applicants than him for the vacancies we had at that moment. I scheduled second interviews with the area managers for other candidates and placed the Cuban rafter's application in the waiting list file. Two days later, fate had it that one of the candidates interviewed for the second time didn't meet the expectations of the area managers. They asked me to look for a replacement promptly. I found myself in the pleasant position to make the Cuban fellow happy or at least help him ease some of his worries.

It was almost six in the afternoon on a Thursday when the managers informed me about their need. I walked to my office and took out the rafter's folder to make the phone call. I anticipated the joy of the poor fellow. However, someone hastily reminded me that we had a happy hour in a bar across the street to celebrate a fellow manager's birthday. I was the personnel manager. I had to be a people's person. I couldn't say no to those social events, so I decided to put off the phone call. I would do it first thing in the morning the following day.

18

Roberto Porta-Córdoba

When I got to the office early Friday, I had the traditional dose of thick Cuban coffee that the American managers called "go-go juice" and sat at my desk ready to start my working day. I opened the Cuban rafter's folder, dialed his number, and waited.

-Hello –answered a woman in Spanish.

-Good morning, madam -I said also in Spanish-. I'm calling from "Dawson's Wholesale Club".

A silence followed.

-I need to speak with Mr. Yurisny Hierrezuelo –I informed.

More silence followed.

-Madam? – I said.

I heard a sobbing. Stifled, but clearly audible.

-Madam? –I repeated.

The sobbing turned into a cry.

-Hello? –I insisted.

-I'm sorry –a broken voice said-. What do you want?

-I'm the personnel manager at "Dawson's Wholesale Club" –I repeated, a little confused-. It's important that I speak to Mr. Yurisny Hierrezuelo. There's a good chance we can offer him a job.

The woman cried openly.

-That's not possible –she said, sobbing.

-But… he seemed very interested in a position here –I said.

-It's just that… he can't… he can't… -she said.

-Why not? What happened, madam?

-He died –she said.

I stood up in shock, thinking what a sick joke that was.

19

-Madam –I insisted, baffled, as if I hadn't understood-. I need to speak with him. This is not a prank. It's a real opportunity.

The woman kept sobbing.

-He's dead. He's dead –she repeated.

I was speechless. I didn't know what to say.

-Check the newspaper –she added-. He died yesterday.

-That's alright, madam –I replied-. I'm sorry.

I hung up. I stood in a daze for a few seconds, then I rushed to grab The Miami Herald from my boss's office. That couldn't be true. There had to be a mistake. I checked the local news section and didn't find anything. I checked the entire newspaper, section by section, page by page, the obituaries, the health section, the business section, even the sports section... nothing. Was that woman pulling my leg? Had I dialed the wrong number?

It occurred to me to check the Spanish issue of The Miami Herald. I found one in the employee lounge and I anxiously took it to my office. This better be a prank, I kept thinking. I shut the door and I searched frantically for the news. It didn't take me too long to find it. There, on one of the first pages, was the picture of the Cuban rafter, smiling... happy... alive. I don't recall the header, but I do remember the paragraph of his family describing how anguished and desperate he had been for the past two weeks, and how he had decided to take his life by hanging himself in his room.

The time of the death was estimated at 6:30 p.m. the day before, around the time I was enjoying the happy hour drinks with my coworkers.

20

The Boy with Three Arms

Polymelia is a congenital disorder in which a person is born with more than the usual number of limbs. This was the case of Yasin Beg, a boy born with three arms in the beautiful country of Tajikistan, in Central Asia.

Most cases of polymelia result in the removal of the additional limbs after confirming they are unnourished or dysfunctional. Yasin's case was different. He was born with two perfectly developed right arms, which amazed the doctors and specialists.

The newborn remained at the hospital under observation for several days, in case one of the little arms suffered a necrosis and stopped functioning. Fortunately, Yasin didn't suffer any complications and his parents were able to take him home after two weeks. The news of the boy born with three arms spread all over the country and even made international headlines as a marvel of nature.

Despite his extraordinary condition, Yasin's first months passed normally. He was a healthy and lively baby. His early school years in his hometown of Qurghonteppa were very interesting. His schoolmates reacted with innocent curiosity at Yasin's three arms, but he was never a target of mockery, bullying, or scorn. Other than an occasional reporter asking for an interview or pictures for an article, it could be said that Yasin's childhood was rather normal.

All that changed the day he celebrated his seventh birthday. Among the presents he received, one grabbed his attention: a dutar. This was long-necked

21

lute with only two strings that produced soft and mellow musical sounds. With the help of an uncle, Yasin learned to play the dutar with extraordinary ease and –most importantly- managed to use his third arm to create a combination of tones at a speed and precision never heard before from that instrument.

It didn't take long for Yasin to stand out at his school's musical events. By age 10, he had learned to play other musical instruments like the guitar, the piano, and the drums. He had natural talent, but no doubt he was immensely aided by his third arm. He played known pieces and began composing his own. Soon, local promoters took notice and young Yasin became a fixed feature in concerts and shows around the country of 8 million people. Inadvertently, he also became the second most popular touristic attraction in town. What was the first one?

For years, tourists who visited Tajikistan would make a stop at Qurghonteppa to take their picture next to the so called "House of Ibrahim," an old and dilapidated house in which it was believed that Ibrahim Bek had clandestinely operated. Ibrahim was one of the *basmachi* leaders that had resisted the Bolshevik invasion in the 1920s, when the Soviets started their Central Asia expansion. The respect to the house and its history had been cautiously kept secret by the locals during the years of annexation to the Soviet Union for fear that the Russians would demolish it. To the Tajik, the house –almost in ruins- symbolized the spirit of resistance, the protection of their culture, and the courage of their people during foreign invasions. Now, tourists who visited the city, also started to ask for a picture with Yasin.

22

Despite all the distractions, Yasin never abandoned school, not even when his concert or show schedule became frantic. The arrival of international fame happened suddenly –although not surprisingly- during a cultural presentation in Dushanbe, the capital and largest city. The event was part of the Independence Day festivities and was hosted by the president. Politicians, diplomats, and distinguished foreign guests were in attendance. They were all impressed with Yasin's performance. One of them happened to have connections with a music band in Belgium and didn't hesitate to send them a video of Yasin playing the piano and the guitar.

Only two months later, the 16-year old Yasin and his father traveled to Europe for an audition that would lead to a series of unusual and extraordinary concerts through a dozen cities of the continent. There was no need for much preamble. Seeing a handsome, young, and talented musician with three arms was a unique happening that require little imagination or preparation. Backed up by a modern band and visionary producers, Yasin became an instant sensation.

The breakout success of the humble and charismatic Tajik teenager continued in the United States, where its unparalleled music marketers transformed him into a youth idol with a greatly publicized concert tour, appearances in the highest rated night shows, and invitations to share stage with famous guitar, keyboard, and drum players from all musical genres. How not to love a performer who could sign two autographs at the same time? The medical guild and related interest groups also invited

23

Yasin to forums with the purpose of examining and researching his prodigious physique. All of sudden, polymelia had become a trending topic of which everyone wanted to know about.

The craze in the United States included the sale of sweaters and t-shirts showing three flexing arms, three arms with clenching fist, or three hands making the peace sign. Bootlegged tasteless versions included three arms wrapped around a woman's body or three hands giving the finger. Yasin and his father – converted overnight in advisor and bodyguard- enjoyed the attention and the warm reception from the American public and its vibrant media, but when a show producer obnoxiously insisted that Yasin perform juggling tricks at an aquarium next to an octopus tank, Yasin's father knew it was time to go back home and take a break. Americans were too much.

Unlike other celebrities who found themselves overwhelmed with sudden fame and money, Yasin was able to surf the waves of stardom and wealth without major trouble. Other than some privacy invasion and having to complete his high school online, Yasin's life was not dramatically affected by his abrupt success. He had no problem with drugs, no problem with people, and no problem with controversies. When in Tajikistan, he made a point of performing for free, gearing his shows separately to children, youth, and adults. He became a national pride.

With his father always by his side, Yasin's agents took him to a lengthy world tour that included Asia, Australia, Africa, and South America. Having already an established name rendered the tour a very

24

profitable venture, allowing the young star to perform in stadium-sized venues, signed lucrative deals, and secure long-term royalties. However, by the time his concerts returned to Europe and the United States, Yasin was getting exhausted and his father was concerned about the frequency of his performances.

He got to play in almost every major U.S. city, with the exception of three: one in Alabama because nativist organizations argued that the exaltation of Yasin's music could promote the uprooting of their own culture; one in California because protesters felt that his Tajik origin made him an anti-Soviet figure with a potentially reactionary and anti-progressive message; and another one in Florida because local promoters and city commissioners ran out of time before they could agree on things like parking fees, ticket taxes, or venue suitability.

It was after this excruciating tour that Yasin complained of numbness in one of his two right arms. The doctors in Tajikistan weren't alarmed at first because they assumed that it was caused by fatigue. Nonetheless, when the numbness turned to tingling and pain, the specialists applied an ultrasound that revealed a small tumor under the innermost right arm. Yasin had to undergo surgery.

Happily, the tumor was not malignant and the doctors successfully removed it, however, bad news arose. The family was informed that the tumor had impaired some of the third arm's ligaments and that the arm was no longer functional. Everyone was stunned. Yasin's parents realized there was no point in having his son walk around with a hanging useless limb.

25

There was no way around it. The third arm was surgically removed.

News of Yasin's surgery traveled fast. He received thousands of get-well-soon cards and messages from inside and abroad. The city mayor paid him a visit at the hospital and the president called him to wish him a speedy recovery and a quick return to music. Yasin felt lucky that the tumor was only a scare, and after resting for a few weeks, he started rehearsing and adapting his instrument playing to a two-arm technique, like a normal musician. Happily for him, his talents and discipline were so good that in a matter of months he was playing the piano, the guitar, and other instruments at a high level. His agents received the go-ahead to assemble a new tour while Yasin played a couple of free local concerts to warm up. But the international calls didn't come.

His father contacted some of the promoters he had met in Europe and Asia, but, suddenly, the interest for Yasin had vanished. The agents tried to book him at different musical festivals in the United States and Australia, but received a lackluster response. They also tried to team Yasin up with other stars, but their agents declined citing previous commitments. With the exception of a few TV shows, the abroad demand for Yasin's act had dried out. One morning, in the large and beautiful house Yasin had bought for his family, he stood shirtless in front of a mirror. He looked at himself. He only had two arms. He looked bizarre. He looked abnormal. He felt like a freak.

Coincidentally with Yasin's twist of fate, the House of Ibrahim had to be demolished. A wall and part of the old roof had collapsed during a minor

26

earthquake, and the city government had no choice but tearing it down for public safety. The influx of tourists to Qurghonteppa waned considerably. And when they learned that the famed pictures with Yasin shaking two hands at the same time were no longer possible, it waned even more. In a single month, the city had lost two of its main attractions

Yasin's stardom was fleeting, but abundant and merciful enough to guarantee him and his family financial security for life. He completed his transition to adulthood a wise and caring man, and also a grateful one. One evening, as he stared at the lifeless ruins of the former House of Ibrahim on his way to promote a local charity, he touched the lifeless scars of his former third arm, and smiled. He knew the difference.

Roberto Porta-Córdoba

Between Earth and Heaven

I finally got to publish my poetry book. As part of the publishing house services, I was interviewed by the main local newspapers, attended some TV shows, and went to some radio programs. The book was titled "Between Earth and Heaven". Many friends attended its presentation and purchased it. My family was proud, but it was my seven-year-old son the first one to set off the alarm.

-I'm not going to read your book –he said the following day of the presentation.

-Why not?

-Because it's boring.

-How do you know it's boring?

-Because the lady on TV said that it had 400 pages, and that is boring.

Actually, the book was thick. For some reason, the publishers reduced its trim size at the last minute and to avoid increasing the number of pages, they ordered the printer to reduce the margins. The design suffered a bit and the result was a tight book, packed with long paragraphs and no art, except its attractive cover. When the book hit the bookstores, sales were slow.

My wife Idalia gave me another fateful signal. The first nights, before going to sleep, I watched her read my book with interest. She would place it on her night table, on top of a book by John Grisham. I felt flattered when I noticed the page marker go deeper into my book, but soon I started to notice how the page marker moved slower and slower, until it stopped

29

halfway through the book. Silently, I watched how one morning the John Grisham book was on top of mine and how eventually my wife stopped leaving my book on her nigh table and moved it to a small rack in front of our toilet, where we placed old magazines and books about fitness, health, and similar subjects.

Taken aback, but not willing to show it, I surreptitiously placed my book on the bed the night my wife was packing for a business trip out of town. I figured that with all the airport waiting she could resume her reading of it. I was deeply disappointed when after dropping her off at the airport the following morning, I found my book laying on her dressing table. She had only taken the John Grisham book.

That same afternoon, my brother called me to inform me that it had been decided. Several cousins and friends had organized a party to celebrate the 80 years of uncle Boris and they needed to know if we could be the hosts.

-When is the party? –I asked.

-Friday, the day after tomorrow.

-Idalia won't be here –I said-, but if you help me with the details…

-No worries –my brother said. We got your back. We'll take care of everything. Your house is big and close to everybody.

Later that day, one of my cousins called me to fill me in. They would bring mariachis, a wind band, and a DJ. I hesitated a bit about hosting a party this big in the absence of Idalia, but since they insisted that they would handle everything –including the cleanup- I gave my consent.

30

My cousin Henry told me with a chuckle that they had a surprise in store for uncle Boris. Since he'd been a widow for the last 6 years, his many nephews wanted to bring him one of those large cakes with a sexy dancer inside. They had consulted with their wives and everyone felt that it would be something innocent and fun for uncle Boris. Despite his old age, the good man had always kept his sense of humor and a flash of mischief in his eyes.

On Friday afternoon, I took our son to his best friend's house for a sleepover. This would be an adult party, he would probably get bored and, besides, I didn't like the idea of him seeing a semi naked woman come out of a giant cake. Henry, one of our cousins' husband was in charge of hiring a dancer from a local strip club.

By nightfall, my house was a hive of people. Around 30 guests, between relatives and close friends, had rented plastic chairs, decorated the entrance with colorful balloons, packed the bar, put out trays of snacks, and set dining tables on the backyard. Luckily, our house was spacious, and there was plenty of parking on the street.

While my brother and the others took care of the logistics, I made sure uncle Boris had everything he needed and that he was having a good time. Idalia called me and I put him on the phone for her to wish him a happy birthday. She apologized for missing the occasion and promised to visit him when she came back from her trip.

As planned, around 10 pm, Henry showed up with the dancing girl. Whispering, he explained to us that the girl at the strip club wanted to charge too much

31

and that he'd had to resort to a sexual worker he found around the club, which charged much less. I totally disliked the idea. However, the party was in motion and I didn't want to rain on everyone's parade. We had the girl come in through the backyard, where we had a small private terrace with access to the main bedroom. The cardboard support for the cake had been assembled earlier by my brother and he'd left it in there, the only place where no one could see it. My brother instructed the girl to remain hidden inside the cake support until we rolled it outside and he gave her the signal to burst out. The girl was not too tall, but when she removed her clothes and flaunted her lingerie and stockings, everyone noticed her scented brunette complexion and her voluptuous curves.

While exiting the room to prepare the surprise act, I had a bad hunch followed by a sudden attack of morality. It was obvious that the girl was of humble origins, and although prostitution was still rampant in our town, I couldn't help feeling complicit of an exploitation of some kind. Also, I recalled a fatal accident in Italy, in which a young dancer had not jump out of cake at the signaled time and was found dead, suffocated inside the framework. Apparently, the organizers did not leave enough ventilation in the hulk and delayed her exit for too long. I felt the party's vibe was not good anymore.

-Did you guys leave enough ventilation for the girl? -I asked as I closed the door to the room.

-Yes –answered my brother-, don't worry!

-Uncle Boris is going to drool! -added Henry.

One of my cousins asked the wind band to stop playing and announced with great solemnity that we

32

had a surprise for our dear uncle. Then, everyone, including the few who knew about the dancing act and those who knew nothing, began to gather in the large living room from which all furniture had been removed. Uncle Boris, with a glass of rum and coke in his hands and his usual vitality, was called to the front. Some cousins and their wives were scattered around the garden immersed in lively conversations, so they took several minutes to approach. Heriberto, another one of my cousins, decided to take the floor before unveiling the surprise. Woozy with whiskey, he began to toast uncle Boris, stretching it into a kind of biography, interrupted every ten seconds by cheering and the spontaneous comments of the rowdy group of relatives.

I began to get restless when my cousin Santiago, the eldest of uncle Boris' sons, also decided to address his father and elaborate about his virtues. He was followed by Sonia, his sister. I looked at my watch. Fifteen minutes had gone by since we left the girl inside the giant cake. Someone else proposed yet another toast, preceded by a lengthy speech. Other relatives asked for an ovation for uncle Boris which extended the wait to twenty minutes.

Finally, to my relief, Henry and my brother walked to the room to bring the giant cake. When they reappeared rolling the large table and support, the DJ started playing disco music and the party resumed. Everybody anticipated the surprise and some of my female cousins grabbed uncle Boris and moved him closer to the cake right in the middle of the living room. Everything was ready. I forgot about my demureness for a moment and joined the fuss.

33

My brother gave the signal to the dancing girl with a couple of knocks on the cake cardboard. Nothing happened. He repeated the knocks while laughing like a naughty boy. The bash and the music were at their peak, but the girl didn't come out. My fun turned into anguish when I saw Henry knocked on the back of the cake support without any response. Horrified, I gave someone the drink I was holding and ran towards the cake. I feared the worst. With my heart in my throat, I demanded the cake top to be removed. My brother –by now confused- shouted into of the support's openings, but the girl still didn't come out. The others realized something was wrong and stopped dancing to see what was happening. We finally removed the cake top. There was no one inside...

The crowd of cousins and relatives began to whistle and boo. Uncle Boris was puzzled, smiling, and having no clue about what was going on. Henry, my brother, and I looked at each other in panic. The space was empty. There was no one inside the cake. How could it be?

I walked quickly to my room. I thought that maybe the girl needed to use the toilet and had left her position inside the cake just as the guys had rolled it out of the room. Then I noticed. Our dresser's drawers were opened and empty. Henry and my brother walked in seconds later. My disheveled face must have surprised them.

The mischievous dancing girl had left by the same route she had come in. She had taken all of our valuables: jewelry, watches, a smartphone, a tablet, a laptop, cash, and other stuff. She had swept us clean.

34

Roberto Porta-Córdoba

Our nigh tables' drawers were also emptied. The thief must have used a large plastic bag my wife had in the bedroom to throw in there everything she found. Her skills amazed me. She even had time to empty out the ornate shelves on the wall and raze through the toiletries and personal care items we kept in the bathroom. Henry and my brother left the room to alert everyone.

I was ready to call the police, but then a feeling of atonement took hold of me. I stopped and stood there in silence. Maybe I deserved this. Somehow it felt like poetic justice. I had lent myself to this charade with the girl. This was payback time. I put my phone away and started to open the door, but something caught my eye.

I noticed that an antique music box and some miniature bronze figures that my wife kept on her dressing table were also gone. Everything was gone, except my book. The book was there! The only thing the slick crook had consciously left behind. And I say consciously because she had even taken the fashion catalog and the old magazines that were under it, as if she had picked just what she wanted to take with her. She didn't take my book! A wave of rage came over me. I retracted my previous morals and launched a string of expletives against her. When I smelled her cheap perfume on the book cover, that was it for me. I got furious and called the police.

Fictions of an Immigrant

Roberto Porta-Córdoba

Around the World in 1080 days

Antonio Pigafetta was an Italian nobleman and scholar who took part in the sea expedition that circumnavigated the Earth between 1519 and 1522, organized and captained by the Portuguese sailor Ferdinand Magellan.

There's no need to detail how Pigafetta managed to enlist in the expedition with the title of supernumerary. Suffice it to say that he worked in Spain for influential personalities who were close to the Crown and that he was attracted to adventure, writing, and the possibility of reaching posterity. Without question, Pigafetta accomplished all these goals. His writings composed a detailed journal of the epic voyage and his name was immortalized with the posthumous publication of his notes in a book titled "The first voyage around the world".

It is through his notes that we know that Magellan set sail from Cádiz, Spain on September 20, 1519, commanding five vessels and 239 men, attempting to find an alternate route to the Maluku islands, source of the spices highly coveted in Europe.

Through Pigafetta we learned how Magellan – like Christopher Columbus- insisted in finding that alternate route westward, trying to find a passage through the huge continent recently discovered. Thanks to his journal we know how the experienced captain led his fleet through the cold waters of the

37

South Atlantic before finally discovering the passage that today bears his name: the Strait of Magellan.

Because of Pigafetta we also know about the suffering and starvation endured by the crew after entering the Pacific Ocean, which forced them to eat rats marinated with sawdust and boiled leather until they were able to reach land three months later.

And thanks to Pigafetta, we also learned how Magellan encountered death in the Philippines while fighting 1500 Cebuano natives with only 49 of his men in the battle of Mactan. The writer tells this episode with abundant details, describing the gallantry of Magellan and how he covered the retreat of his men, despite being wounded, before heroically falling to the cutlasses and spears of the warriors. Without leaving aside the respect and sorrow felt for his captain, Pigafetta writes about the success of the commercial trade established in the Maluku islands –which was the main objective of the endeavor- and then narrates the return of the expedition to Spain, now under the command of Juan Sebastian Elcano, in one single vessel and with only 18 survivors, on September 6, 1522.

The first thing Pigafetta did upon returning was to visit the churches of Our Lady of Victory and of Saint Mary the Ancient in Seville, with a candle in hand and barefooted, fulfilling a promise made together with the other survivors. He later left for Valladolid where he met with His Majesty King Charles I and offered him a rendering of his manuscript. He eventually returned to Italy and devoted himself to the Grand Master of the Knights of Rhodes, to whom he handed another rendering of the manuscript.

But it's here where things get tangled up for the modern historian. The aforementioned book published posthumously with Pigafetta's notes was based on the manuscript that he handed to the Grand Master, the one where Magellan's death is regarded as heroic. The manuscript handed to the king has never been found. However, a version with the signature of Pigafetta turned up recently at a private library in Valladolid. Upon close inspection, scholars believe that this manuscript is the one Pigafetta presented to King Charles I.

What is striking about this finding is that when comparing both manuscripts there is a major difference in one crucial passage: the death of Magellan. In the pages recently found, the heroic version described by Pigafetta is nowhere to be found, there's no reference to any battle of Mactan, nor to any brave sacrifice made by Magellan.

Instead, the notes describe how that the captain attended a friendly invitation from Lapu-Lapu, ruler of Mactan Island, along with 49 of his most loyal men. This would help explain why Magellan dared to battle against 1500 natives in such a disadvantageous number. The manuscript narrates how Lapu-Lapu, impressed with the artillery, weapons, and power of

Fictions of an Immigrant

the visitors, took Magellan for a god and prepared a ceremony to present him to his tribe.

Part of the elaborated ritual, enlivened with flutes and drums, consisted of the new "god" smelling and approving several food samples prepared by his new "faithful". The manuscript also tells us that one of these foods had a really penetrating smell which caused Magellan to go into an unstoppable sneezing fit that halted the ceremony completely. Unfortunately for the Portuguese captain, sneezing was not common in the Cebuano culture and it occurred mostly in women; sneezing was not considered too manly and certainly not divine. Gods didn't sneeze. A couple of sneezes signaled the arrival of a woman's menstrual period and three or four meant that bad things could come over the woman's family; a sneezing fit, however, meant only one thing: the sneezer was calling upon evil spirits.

Lapu-Lapu and his startled entourage must have been furious with this disappointing and mixed display of feebleness and devilry. The manuscript details how Magellan was immediately apprehended after the initial laughter of the crowd turned into fear, and how the was slaughtered like an animal while his companions desperately rowed back to the ships under a rain of arrows. Since it was to be a friendly gathering, only three of them were carrying firearms. The report concludes this unfortunate episode revealing that Magellan was still sneezing while the natives tore off his limbs and pulled out his intestines.

40

If the manuscript is verified authentic, what moved Pigafetta to change the original version afterwards? Why would he give the humiliating version to the king before modifying it later for the scholars of Rhode? An early speculation could be that the respect and admiration Pigafetta felt for his captain didn't allow him to stain his accomplishments with such an unfit and degrading incident. Another possibility is that since Magellan was Portuguese, the writer thought that the Spanish monarch wouldn't mind learning about his disgrace since the maritime rivalry between Portugal and Spain was fierce.

Regardless of any possible motives, the work of Antonio Pigafetta, -the Italian nobleman from Vicenza, who voluntarily turned into a scribe for a total of 1080 days- will serve as the best legacy to humanity of this historical journey.

Roberto Porta-Córdoba

Visiting John Lennon

I grew up listening to the Beatles music. They were very popular in Greece and my siblings were ardent fans. Although I wouldn't say they were my favorite band, I strongly believe that their influence on contemporary music and their contribution to the pop and rock genres are historically unmatched. So, when I had the opportunity to travel to the United States and visit New York City for the first time, I didn't hesitate to include in my itinerary a quick stopover at the John Lennon's memorial in Central Park. Just like I admire Paul McCartney for his beautiful musical arrangements, I admired Lennon for his passionate and philosophical lyrics.

For many, New York is the quintessential large city, the embodiment of excess and intensity, the provenance of sight and sound, the Big Apple. I'm convinced that those who unwillingly ignore the magnificence of New York are probably the same ones who unwillingly ignore the magnificence of the Beatles, the same ones who ignore that the Great Wall of China it's not really visible from space, the same ones who ignore that fingernails don't really keep growing after death, and the same ones who ignore that eating eggs everyday isn't really bad for your heart. But, why do they ignore all this? I think that it's only a lack of intellectual curiosity, a lack of desire to read one extra paragraph, a lack of desire to listen to one extra phrase, a lack of desire to pause and contemplate life for one extra minute.

The memorial is a nice garden in Central Park known as Strawberry Fields, named after the Beatles' song of the same name. It was built in front of the Dakota Apartments building, where Lennon was killed in 1980. Several countries donated trees to draw attention to its simple and natural beauty: Canada sent maple trees, Holland sent daffodils, Israel sent cedars, and the Soviet Union sent birches. Also, Princess Grace of Monaco sent rabbits, while artisans from the city of Naples sent white and black tiles to replicate a mosaic of ancient Pompeii with the word "Imagine" in the center. The memorial is really beautiful and is considered a "garden for peace". The most practical way to reach this place is by taking the subway and getting off at the station on 72 street and Central Park West. It was outside of this station where I met Lamar, a peculiar character I must talk about.

Lamar was a black fellow about 6'7" and 260 pounds, impossible to miss, even among the crowd of people going down and up the stairs. He was a homeless man, one of the half-million indigents prowling in the most powerful country of the world. And yet, Lamar was not a beggar. He didn't like to panhandle. No, sir. Lamar was a proud man and believed in earning his bread with the sweat of his brow. I calculated his age at about 35.

When we exited the subway, my buddies and I decided to enjoy one of those tasty sidewalk hotdogs.

While we ate, we observed how Lamar helped older people cross the street, how he pointed tourists in the right direction, and how he helped anybody who looked lost. He did it with joy, with zest, almost with delight, and he didn't seem to care much about the coins, the few bills, or the simple thanks he received in exchange. As soon as he saw my black t-shirt with the iconic John Lennon face printed on it, he knew where we were heading.

-Going to visit John? –he said in a hoarse voice-. Follow me dawg!

Lamar's smile, energy, and positive demeanor were contagious. Giving my companions no time to react, he grabbed their backpacks, put them on his shoulders, and began a rant about Lennon and his legacy while he led us to the memorial. Before you could say Alexander the Great, the big man had pushed his way through the crowd and had us looking straight at the mosaic. There were women, men, adolescents, children, hippies, and people of many nationalities gathered around it, many of them also dressed in shirts or clothing allusive to Lennon or the Beatles. The constant click of photo cameras was clearly audible.

Sounding like a consummate scholar, Lamar gave us lecture about the place, including the donation of the trees, the gift from Naples, the rabbits, and other details we already knew, but also others that I ignored, such as Yoko Ono –Lennon's widow- donating a million dollars for the works, that the name of the architect was Bruce Kelly, that a man named Gary dos

45

Fictions of an Immigrant

Santos decorated the mosaic with flowers everyday, thus earning the nickname "mayor of Strawberry Fields", that the rabbits donated had been all female, and several other anecdotes.

While Lamar took a picture of our group posing around the mosaic, I noticed a large scar on his forehead. It had the shape of an "X", as if someone had branded the poor man. Risking indiscretion, I asked him how he'd gotten it. With a loud laugh, Lamar confided to us that it had happened long ago, in a street fight against a rival gang. He didn't seem to care much about it and continued guiding us through the rest of the nice garden until it was time for him to go.

-I gotta go, dawg! –Lamar said in his hoarse voice-. Gotta take care of other people!

We thanked him for his time and tipped him well. He walked away happy and with all the vitality of the world, as if the spirit of John Lennon had recharged him.

To wrap up the visit, I prompted my friends to cross back the avenue and take a picture at the entrance of the Dakota building.

-What for? –they asked.

-What do you mean "what for"? –I replied.

-Let's go back downtown, it's getting late –one of them said.

-Okay, but let's take those pictures first –I insisted.

I explained to them that my interest for the picture at the entrance of the Dakota was because it

46

had been precisely there where Lennon had received the shots that killed him, and also because it was one of the most exclusive apartment buildings in New York.

-How exclusive? –they asked.

-So exclusive that celebrities like Madonna, Cher, and Carly Simon were turned down as occupants –I said.

My buddies laughed at me, but obliged to take my picture. None of them wanted to take one of themselves. They didn't know about the incident. They couldn't care less. I ignored their sneer and –after asking the guard at the entrance for permission- I solemnly had my picture taken at the entrance of the Dakota. Some pedestrians looked at me in puzzlement. I just couldn't process it. How was it possible that no one knew that at this famous site a fanatic had taken the life of one of the most iconic musicians of our time? Had no one heard or read about how the mad killer had calmly surrendered and even waited for police to arrive at the scene? Had no one watched on TV the thousands of people gathering along that street after hearing the news of the tragedy? It was broadcasted all around the world! I felt bummed out. Was my compulsion a Greek thing? Maybe, but my companions were Greek, too!

It was the time of roll film cameras. Digital cameras were not around yet. There was no way to immediately verify the quality of the pictures taken, so it was until I flew back home that I discovered that

47

none of the three pictures my buddies had taken of me at the Dakota were good. They all came out blurry or dark. I was disheartened. How could that happen? I resigned myself to think that I would take them again when I returned to New York in the future, but I couldn't resign myself to the thought that none, absolutely none of my friends, relatives, or coworkers, knew that the shocking murder of John Lennon had taken place at that famous building. How could it be?

Destiny had it that I had to wait 25 years to go back to the *Big Apple*. I never thought it would take me that long. Taking advantage of a business trip, I stayed the weekend in the city and I made sure to visit places I missed the first time, and revisit my favorite landmarks, including of course the memorial to John Lennon.

I got off the subway at the same station on 72 street and Central Park West. This time, my only companions were my smartphone and a selfie stick. The world had changed, but the memorial's surroundings had not. Other than the higher price of the sidewalk hotdogs, everything looked the same as the first time. I breathed in the cool autumnal air of New York and sipped a hot chocolate while looking in the direction of the memorial across the avenue. This time, I would make sure to take my picture at the entrance of the Dakota. I felt good. Suddenly, I spotted something that made me pause.

Crossing the avenue in my direction, I saw a big black man gesticulating and laughing with an

48

elderly couple. Could that be…? No way! But when he walked by me I could clearly see the scar with the shape of an "X" on his forehead. For the life of Zeus, it was Lamar! I was in shock.

It was impossible not to say hello. He first turned around with a perplexed face. I tried to remind him of my visit to memorial 25 years before. The good man resumed his smile and told me he would be back in a minute after he guided the couple to the subway turnstile. His hoarse voice was the same. I stood there in awe with the hot chocolate in my hand. It was the same black giant, the very same as two decades ago, although now with gray hair on his galloping baldness, a slower walk, and a protuberant belly.

-So, what's your name, sir? –he said upon returning.

It was obvious he had no idea who I was, but correctly discerned that I was there to pay tribute to John Lennon.

-Fixing to visit John? –he said with his big smile.

As kindly as the first time, he offered to guide me to the memorial. When I mentioned to him our previous meeting, Lamar opened his eyes wide and, sounding apologetic, said he didn't remember. I let him tell me everything I already knew about the memorial, although he provided new details. He told me the Strawberry Fields "mayor" had passed away and that after 9/11 many vigils for the victims had been organized there. His enthusiasm was the same, but he

49

looked tired and panted a little as we walked toward the mosaic. To my dismay, I learned he was still homeless. I still couldn't believe I was chatting with him after such a long time. The man was an authentic expert on the Beatles, John Lennon, and the memorial at Central Park. With the years, his arsenal of information had expanded. He would refer in detail to previous visits of famous people, anniversary celebrations, and the minor changes to the garden. Indeed, Lamar rendered his anecdotes with a true sense of vocation, conveying a true sense of customer service, a true sense of excellence.

And then, the moment arrived. After taking a selfie with my old acquaintance and treating him to a couple of hotdogs, I told him I needed to go to the Dakota. Lamar looked at me with an expressionless face. I thought that maybe he didn't want to deviate from his usual route.

-But, you don't have to come with me –I said.

-Are you staying in that building, sir? –he asked.

-No –I answered laughing-. I wished!

-So, why do you wanna go there? –he asked.

A strange feeling of solitude began to invade me.

-Well -I said-. To take a picture at the entrance… where John was shot.

Lamar's tired eyes opened wide again while he looked in the direction of the Dakota.

Roberto Porta-Córdoba

-Whaaaaaaaaaaaaaaaaaat? For real, sir? —he yelled.

He didn't know. Lamar didn't know. The man who had been walking the area for more than thirty years, pacing on those streets, covering every inch of those sidewalks, seven days a week, the four stations of the year... didn't know.

It was me then who guided the big man to the entrance of the Dakota Apartments. I told him that the murderer's name was Mark David Chapman; that Lennon had signed an autograph for him on the same sidewalk, hours before; that the shooter had waited for his return in the vicinity, casually flipping through a book titled "Catcher in the Rye"; and that he was still serving a life sentence despite pledging insanity.

-That's awesome... awesome! —Lamar kept repeating in total excitement-. I'll start telling my tourists! Thanks for sharing! Awesome! They're gonna love it, sir!

This time, I was able to take my picture at the entrance. Needless to say, it came out... awesome!

Roberto Porta-Córdoba

Dreams in Pennsylvania

To say that love conquers all sounds cliché, and also inaccurate. And sometimes, not only sounds inaccurate, it *is* inaccurate. In the case of our dear Lisa, it would be more appropriate to say that love risks it all.

The five of us became friends back in the 70s, those ancient times when you could not "follow" or "unfollow" a person with a simple click. We met during the Equal Rights Amendment heyday, when women marched to fight for their legal right to equality. Although we came from different towns of Pennsylvania, we attended the same nearby college and literally jumped in the same wagon of the "freedom train" to Illinois for our first protest march.

I don't know if our movement finally succeeded or not, but I do know that we kept our promise to stay in touch after graduation. All of us – except Lisa- got married and continued to live in Pennsylvania. At first, we would meet every week. Then, when children arrived, we would meet every other week, but we always did. Our friendship was planted in times of comradeship fertility and we took the scheduling of our meetings seriously. We loved each other.

Lisa was an only child. The pride of her parents. They owned a small shop and worked tirelessly. Lisa rewarded them by always being an outstanding student in school and valedictorian in college. She was also hardworking and in a few years she made the business grow. Eventually, she forced her

53

parents to retire and took over the venture. Nobody could ask for a more caring daughter.

Since the beginning, Lisa was in charge of confirming our attendance to the meetings, as well as reminding us who was hosting and what snacks we were to bring. Her known propensity for order and planning made her perfect for the role, just like she had been the perfect tutor or mentor for overwhelmed students in college.

Besides her obsession with organization and compliance, Lisa had two traits: one that concerned us, and one that amused us. We were concerned about her emotional solitude. She had social skills and was an affable person, but her closest companions besides the four of us were her parents. She lived with them and made sure they were never unattended. Twice a year, she would send them in a tour or a cruise. She made sure they enjoyed the twilight of their lives, even if that meant postponing the dawning of her own.

We were amused by her dreams. Although Lisa got up early for work Monday thru Saturday, she slept in on Sunday, making her dreams easier to remember during that extra hour of fat pillows and leisure. Lisa's dreams from Sunday became one of the most anticipated topics of our meetings. We held our breath in suspense when it was her turn to talk and enjoyed every minute of her detailed descriptions. Sometimes we laughed, sometimes we tried to interpret the dreams, sometimes we panicked.

Although Lisa was charming and very dear to us, we never abused her trust by querying about her singleness. During the college years, she got to share with us a couple of flitting romances she tried to

54

harbor without success. One with a boy, one with a girl. More recently, she had confessed that she would love to complement her professional and financial prosperity with a partner, a man who could fill her heart and soul, but also her mind and senses.

Several times we joked with Lisa about possible escapades. We introduced her to several of our husbands' friends. Some devoted single men, some divorced. One of us even had the audacity to organize her a fanciful date with a widow from Silicon Valley. But our dear friend wouldn't budge. They always ended up disappointing her. We decided not to insist.

Lisa's dreams were diverse and original. In one, she could gallop on top of a giant sheep to escape a pursuing malicious snake; in another, she would face an angry crowd demanding a specific product to be carried in her store; or in another, she would panic after forgetting the lyrics to the national anthem in front of a packed hockey arena in Pittsburgh. However, in all of the dreams she would come out triumphant. She would always prevail. We couldn't stop laughing when she would admit pausing her escape from a zombie in a lonely aisle just to correct a misspelled word on a wall, or deviating the course of her boat on a beautiful lake just to pick up a plastic bag some knucklehead had thrown in the water. Her sense of responsibility and righteousness had given Lisa the ability to prolong her dreams at will, enduring dangerous or frantic situations even when aware that she could solve the dilemma just by waking up. With Lisa, there were no shortcuts, no easy way out, even when dreaming. Whatever was started had to be finished, and finished the right way.

55

For the last two months, her dreams had acquired an unusual romantic and rogue ambiance. A handsome man began to appear repeatedly in her dreams. Lisa described him as a manly and refined individual. She told us that the man always appeared towards the end of her dreams, after she had overcome all the dangers. She felt that the man was not a savior, but rather a reward for her troubles. With childish enthusiasm, Lisa told us that she liked the mysterious man, that he had exquisite brown eyes, and that his appearance made her wake up feeling safer and happier. We got excited with all the possible meanings. Premonitions of a love to come? We began to swim in a morbid pond of speculation.

Lisa spoke more and more about the images of the man that she saw in the jungles, desserts, mountains, streets, and creeks of her dreams. With a playful push from us, she admitted that what she now hated most about waking up was having to say goodbye to the man. Her man. We realized what was happening, but we played along despite an ominous feeling of apprehension. We loved our friend, so we also played along when she told us that she now delayed her escape from the dangers in her dreams until the last second, so she could spend more time with the mysterious man.

Maybe that was why the news didn't completely surprise us. One Sunday morning, her maid called us. She was scared. She wanted us to come to the house. Lisa's parents were out of town in one of their biannual tours. A doctor waited in the porch. He was straight with us: our friend had died of sleep apnea. It was the official cause of death. But we knew

56

Roberto Porta-Córdoba

better. We knew our friend. We knew what had happened.

The body was facing up, in pinkish stamped pajamas that matched the bed cover and the slippers from the previous night. Her eyes were softly closed, the sheets were a little scrambled, and her peaceful face revealed a subtly wonderful rogue smile.

Roberto Porta-Córdoba

Bad Confessions

Latin America, how long must we suffer you? How long must we remember your thunderous beauty? The sounds, the colors, the aromas, the cravings? How long must we pretend we no longer long for you? For it is only in Latin America where this episode could've taken place. It happened as recently as last month, but it could've happened as recently as yesterday. Who knows? Nobody has known for over 500 years. What is common knowledge, and sad old news by now, is that the modern plague didn't spare any nation. The silent pandemic challenged all governments and their institutions. No exceptions. It was an exercise in macabre democracy. Perfect globalization.

It was in one of these countries, right in the belly button of the continent, where an older man, with a robust pear belly, entered the church looking for father Alfonso. The man had just lost his job as an accountant after his employer of 15 years had to reduce personnel because of the financial burden imposed by the plague. He was in no mood to fill out any forms, but consented to wear the face mask that the government had begun handing out after several of its cabinet members and hundreds of people had succumbed to the virus. By this time, walking outside without the bothersome mask felt almost like walking in underwear.

-What do you need father Alonso for? –asked a young nun, the voice muffled by her mask.

-Confession –said the man, with a disgruntled gesture.

-Perfect timing –she said-. He's about to finish for today.

The pious woman led the man to a bench near a wooden confessional, but he hesitated.

-Is there any way to confess face-to-face, like in a room, for example? –he asked.

-Sure –replied the nun-. If you don't mind waiting until he's done with the last person.

-Thank you –said the man-. I got bad knees and I also feel more comfortable talking to him like that.

The nun smiled and walked away to escort out a tall, elegant lady, who had come out of the church office behind the altar, accompanied by an older nun. Despite the face masks, the lady's fine perfume left an invisible trail as she walked by to get into the luxurious car waiting for her outside. The older man took a seat on a bench, at a cautious distance from two women who also waited for confession with their masks on. One of the women was reading a psalms book, while the other stared at a sculpture of Saint Sebastian on the wall and caressed her nose over the mask, as if trying to hold on to the essence left by the elegant lady.

After a short while, both women were done and father Alfonso came out of the confessional. He was an old and rather frail looking man, full of white thin air that seemed disproportioned to the size of his pale face and his hollow eyes. The young nun approached him and let him know about the older man's request. The

60

priest nodded in approval and invited the faithful to follow him to his office. His face mask was green and resembled those used by surgeons in an operating room.

-How can I help you, my son? —said the man of the cloth, while unavoidably catching sight of the man's protuberant pear belly.

-Thank you for receiving me, father —said the man, while the young nun closed the door to give them privacy.

-Do you want to confess? —asked father Alfonso.

The older man looked nervous. He scratched his forehead while looking down.

-Yes, father – he nodded.

Father Alfonso looked at him in the eyes and waited for a few seconds.

-You have to say "Bless me, father, for I have sinned" –the priest said.

The old man smiled slightly and blushed.

-How long ago was your last confession? – asked the priest.

The man looked down and cleared his throat.

-Oh, it's been a long time, father.

-How long? Months, years?

-I'm not sure. Maybe a year —said the older man.

Father Alfonso leaned forward and told him not to worry. He made him relax by sharing that many of the faithful who came to his church hadn't confessed in a long time, either. He also reassured him by saying that he cared more about his sins and the sincerity of his repentance than the protocol. The man felt more at ease.

-Father... I understand that you cannot tell my sins to anyone else, is that right?

-Sure, my son. I cannot and I won't.

-Not even if they're really...bad sins, father?

The priest looked up at him.

-No, son. Not even if they're really bad sins – he answered.

The man looked anxious again. He squirmed in his chair.

-I... I... just don't know, father.

-Don't worry –said the priest-, the Seal of Confession won't let me share your sins with anyone.

-What is that? –asked the man-, looking embarrassed.

-It's the duty that all priests have not to disclose whatever you confess to them –said father Alonso-. I cannot tell anyone, absolutely anyone, about anything you reveal to me during confession.

The old man lifted his head and sighed.

-Not even to the police? –he asked.

-Not even to the police – the priest answered.

-If that's the case, father... I confess to you... that I have stolen.

-Go on, son, go on –said father Alonso.

-I also confess that I will steal again –he continued.

Roberto Porta-Córdoba

The priest looked up at him with a puzzled face.

-What do you mean, son?

The old man got up from his chair and took out a gun from under the back of his shirt. He aimed it to the priest's chest. Father Alfonso moaned in shock.

-I'm sorry, father –said the man-. I need all the cash you have in here.

The priest became pale, his hollowed eyes opened up in horror, his jaw dropped while trying to hold his face mask with his hand.

-Quick, father-whispered the man, looking more restless-. I don't want to hurt you.

Father Alfonso took a step to the side. He was trembling and totally confused. He removed his face mask to catch his breath.

-But, son… -he said, while glancing at the door-. How do you know I have cash in this office?

The old man didn't look nervous anymore. He kept pointing the gun at the priest.

-I know you do, father, because your main donors come on Tuesday, and I know the lady who walked out just a while ago - he said-. She brings her entire family's alms for church every week, and I know it's a lot of money.

Father Alfonso dropped his mask on the floor. The man made an attempt to pick it up, but stopped suddenly.

-Sorry, father -he said -. Please hurry up.

-Yes, yes... -answered the priest, without having a clue where to go.

-Hurry! – repeated the man in a hushed voice.

The priest was struggling to catch his breath. He couldn't speak.

-Go to that wardrobe! –the man said, while pointing with his empty hand-. They usually keep the offerings in there.

-How... how... how do you know? –babbled the terrified priest.

-Because that's where father Daens keeps them in his church –he answered.

Father Alfonso looked at the man in disbelief while walking toward the wooden chest in a corner of the office.

-You know father Daens? –he asked.

-Yes! –the man said, holding a finger up to his lips as if shushing him-. I took his alms earlier today, and that's where he'd hidden them.

Father Alfonso opened the chest and found that the man was right. Several envelopes full of cash and bags full of coins were neatly arranged inside.

-You see? –the old man said, while taking a large plastic bag from his back pocket and ordering father Alfonso to put the cash inside.

Father Alfonso unfolded the plastic bag and in less than 30 seconds all the alms were in the bag. The old man tied it with a big knot and lifted his face mask a little. He was sweating.

-Thank you, father –he said, still in a hushed voice-. You were faster than father Daens. He kept asking me why I was taking the alms from his church.

-And why is that, son? –asked the priest a little relieved when the old man quickly put the gun in his back and covered it with his shirt.

-Because I need to, father –he answered, while hurrying to the door-. I got laid off. No one will hire me at my age. I'm ruined. My family has nothing.

Father Alfonso remained standing next to the wooden chest, perplexed, feeling a strange mix of pity and fear.

-And sorry about the gun –added the man before opening the door-. She's my Seal of Confession. I hope you understand.

The priest looked him in the eyes, and then at his pear belly.

-I didn't get my absolution –the man said.

Father Alfonso remained silent, stunned, as if in a dream. He then realized he had peed his pants.

-Never mind, just forgive me father – said the man, before bowing his head and rushing out of the office.

For three consecutive weeks, 16 different priests were robbed at gunpoint in the province, for a total estimate of 10,000 dollars.

The frightening requests for confession ended as abruptly as they had begun, with no suspect ever brought to light. The Seal of Confession was never broken and none of the priests reported the armed

Fictions of an Immigrant

robberies, but one of them noisily fainted at the sight of the gun, triggering an investigation by local police and scaring the robber away.

Roberto Porta-Córdoba

We Need to Talk About It

For several weeks, I knew it would happen. I woke up around the same time, between three and four in the morning, when darkness is thickest. I never recalled much about the dream. Faces? No, there was no need for faces. Bodies? No, there was no need for bodies. I only remembered a feeling of disaster permeating throughout the whole dream.

After waking up -sometimes spooked- I drank a glass of water mixed with the absolute certainty that it would happen. Heat dehydrates and harms, but it's more harmful to be conscious that the approaching dawn won't free you from the disaster you're dreaming about. In the end, the water always tasted like iron to me, although the last time, it might have tasted like iron oxide.

The morning of the day it happened, we had all been present at the stone laying ceremony: the Governor and his cabinet; state Representatives; state Senators; men and women of the press; and people, many people. And of course, they had been there: the Grand Duke and the Grand Duchess. The entourage bathed in southern sunshine, and when the fine dust of the road settled down from the warm air, we all savored it and needed to talk about it.

I don't remember if I was invited to the official lunch. Maybe I was, but judging by the many details that now escape my memory, I must have sit far apart from the most important people. I only remember that the Grand Duchess spoke in Spanish to a group of

67

ladies who had come from Florida. They were very fond of her.

For the night reception, I wanted to look sharp. The State House was repainted and decorated for the memorable and solemn occasion. We wanted to look sharp. After all, it was not common that European nobility held official business at a place other than Washington and even less common that it held it at a small and modest state like ours. My new tie stood out at the gala. I knew I had gotten it right from the moment I walked on the parking lot. I received several compliments. The State House –although I already said it was painted- still maintained its Greek Revival style and evoked our local pride and civic virtues. We were proud citizens, indeed. We will need to talk about it.

The reception was held at the main lobby on the second floor, which looked splendid with its stained glass windows, its beautiful carvings, and the interior view of the dome. After the national anthems, the Secretary of State –the only official from D.C. present- was the first one to speak. He welcomed the distinguished guests and introduced the Governor, who was received with a thunderous round of applause. After brief remarks about the endeavor at hand, it was the time to listen to the Grand Duke. He did it in perfect English. He expressed how happy he and the Grand Duchess were to be in our country and how marvelous our state was. He also received a roaring ovation. We'll also need to talk about it.

The formal ceremony ended. Someone complimented my tie. Sandberg, the eternal State House Chief of Protocol, thanked everyone for their presence and kindly invited us to join the Governor on

68

a toast to the good health of the Grand Duke, the Grand Duchess, and their commendable generosity toward our state. Sandberg's bald head and smile shone with pride as he articulated his words in a perfectly trained voice.

The waiters moved around with their trays packed with glasses of red and white wine. Some of the cabinet members and legislators, with their spouses, approached the main table to greet the Governor and the noble couple. I noticed that three protocol hostesses began distributing a memorial parchment of the visit among everyone present. Sandberg beamed with pride. While I sipped my glass of red wine –I never deciphered the sulky taste of white wine-, I noticed that the parchment included a picture of the noble couple and a nice coin that looked like bronze. And then, it began.

The first one to request an autograph was Murphy, our director of social services, followed by Allen, a Republican Representative. A few minutes later, it was the wife of Keller, our director of parks and recreation. She was quickly followed by Harrison, the thin director of employment and workforce. I found those requests unusual. Little by little, a line had formed in front of the main table. The line moved slowly but steadily, first to greet the noble couple and then the Governor and his wife. On the other side of the room, I saw a strange gesture on Sandberg. He was talking to one of his protocol aids. He looked alarmed.

The line grew by the minute. It was happening. My wine acquired a vague metallic taste. I paid more attention and watched how Mrs. Bradley, a Democrat Senator, had reached the main table and just like the

69

others extended her memorial parchment for an autograph. The Duke and the Duchess smiled cordially and signed. Seconds later, it was the turn of McDaniel, the mayor. Without hesitation, he also extended his parchment; he was followed by Robbins, Hopkins, Pearson, a lady I didn't recognize, Leonard, Mrs. Halpin, Guthrie -our director of commerce, who had two parchments-, our director of administration, our director of motor vehicles, one Republican Senator, one Democrat Representative, Mrs. Crowley... all asking for an autograph of the noble couple on their memorial parchment.

Sandberg was livid. He couldn't conceal his anger. He gesticulated softly but firmly toward the line. He gave orders to his protocol hostesses with clenched teeth. It was happening. By now, my wine tasted like iron oxide and I was overcome with the familiar feeling from my dreams. Soon, there was no line anymore, just a pile of suits and night dresses swarming around the perplexed noble couple who now signed the parchments hurriedly and with a perplexed look on their face. The Governor had moved from the main table and distractedly chatted with some legislators, oblivious to what was going on.

I could see a Democrat Senator attempting to break through the human wall. She couldn't. I observed the always competitive Dempsey shamelessly elbow Anderson, his partisan colleague. We need to talk about it. Some cabinet members clumsily stretched their memorial parchments over the others and even offered their pens to the Gran Duke and the Grand Duchess. Others tried to cut through the mob using the palm of their hands as if it was a dagger. When they

70

failed, they would try from a different angle. Sandberg had to intervene without any kind of forbearance. His face was red with wrath, his bald head sweated with embarrassment, his grimacing eyes defied those who dared to continue pushing forward.

-You boorish! You boorish! -he started yelling with a pained voice while trying to dissolve the excited throng of people.

Finally, a protocol aid with a nervous smile on her face announced through the ceiling speakers that the autograph signing had concluded and that everyone needed to move away from the main table. There were audible exhalations of disappointment in the lobby. The Grand Duke looked serious. The Grand Duchess still kept a pinch of empathy on her face. The Governor raised his glass and offered a toast to the noble couple. Very few of us held a glass at that moment. Sandberg bumped into me. He looked at my tie for a second. It was crooked. The man was pale and panting. I realized I also held a parchment and a pen in my hand.

-We need to talk about it- he said.

Roberto Porta-Córdoba

Faithfully Unfaithful

Time is unbending. It glides off like water in our hands; it dissolves like a pile of rocks crushed by a blinding force coming from the remotest nook of the universe. Time won't stop flowing. And with that outflow, some memories get drifted away. I say this because you could put an end to my life before I remember where, in which clinic of this hemisphere, my destiny began to intertwine with hers.

The woman's name was Jacinta, a *boanerense* brunette in her forties. I was a medical supplies vendor back then, married, with a daughter and –according to the nurses and doctors- with a splendid future ahead. "Keep it up, Valderrama, and you could retire at 50", used to tell me Dr. Gautier. "Darn, I chose the wrong career", said Dr. Piazzolla, one of the best therapists in Argentina. "If I had studied marketing and spoke with half of your verbosity, I would be a millionaire", joked Dr. Alberdi.

It wasn't the money what I appreciated most about my job. I swear it wasn't. What I probably relished most about my occupation was that I didn't have to spend time in an office, trapped inside a building, pricked by the ever-moving hands of a clock. I was my own boss, I was independent, I was my own chieftain. As a supplier, I had to visit a dozen of prospects every week. Some in the northern section of the city, some in the south. At times –if the lead was promising- I would venture in other directions. I had

73

the freedom that only believers have. It always paid off.

Jacinta –whom I got to think of as a friend- was undeniably an attractive woman. She had straight, black hair, thin lips, nose chiseled like a Florentine marble sculpture, eyebrows like brushstrokes of coal, and hazel autumnal eyes. Tall and lean, with a pear body shape, it would be accurate to say she was in her physical prime. She was no beauty queen, either, but elegant and sophisticated enough to turn heads everywhere she went.

Yet, there was one thing about her that I found odd, something that stroke me as offbeat. It was her facial expression after laughing at a joke or after wrapping up an issue on which we both agreed. It didn't happen frequently, but when it did, she would look me in the eyes, would erase the smile from her face, and arching her eyebrows would say to me: "thank you, sugar". It only lasted seconds, but during that brief moment I felt as if I could look through her soul, and all I saw was loneliness, but, not any loneliness, rather an abysmal and deluged loneliness. The few times I perceived that expression, Jacinta seemed to enter a profound state of self-absorption. "Thank you, sugar," she would say, and I'd feel a shiver down my spine.

She was a surgeon, with a specialty I never cared to find out. However, she had gradually stopped practicing to dedicate more time to her job as a public health inspector. In Argentina, some bureaucracies still

74

pay. Jacinta kept her clinic, a modest space next to her home, but she limited her services to old patients or ambulatory procedures that didn't require a fully equipped operating room. Like me, she preferred to subordinate her finances to her total freedom. We both despised confinement and subjection to a single place.

Jacinta was divorced. She had wedded at 27 and her marriage had lasted only a couple of years. She never had another formal relationship. I saw her frequently, twice or three times a week. We ran into each other at clinics, health centers, and hospitals. She was immersed in her auditing chores; I was immersed in my selling tactics. At times, we would share a coffee in the waiting rooms of her audited institution or in the waiting rooms of my clients. At the end of the day, they were the same. Same people, different demeanor. Jacinta would face flattery, I would face bargaining. I imagine her looks have something to do with this unequal treatment.

Please believe me when I say that I was always faithful to my wife. I never had any reason not to be. One might be unfaithful when something is lacking at home, but my wife and my daughter provided me with all the emotional and affective arsenal that my ordinary salesman life required. Please believe me that I had everything I wanted at home. How could I then sink into the swamp I'm about to tell you?

Maybe it was a matter of proximity. Despite being younger than her, we had a lot in common. Often, we shared the same subways, the same routes, the same long walks; those close walks where words may acquire a touch of greenish anxiety, of reddish furtive confidence, and sometimes of purple daring. During the rainy season, or when the austral cold began to elbow its way in, we opted for our cars. When the city council regulated vehicle access downtown, she and I started to carpool, to split gas and tolls, and to share time, much more time.

I know it sounds like a tired cliché if I say we didn't realize how our intimacy began. Once again, it was never in my plans to cheat on my wife. In addition to loving her, I always thought that having an affair required to assemble a parallel universe, the adoption of deceiving tactics, and the systematic implementation of lies, excuses, alibis, and precautions. In short, the creation of a fictitious world. It sounded too complicated. We salesmen don't dig metaphysics.

It happened after a medical workshop, at the end of a cloudy afternoon. I was hungry. I always stayed away from the snack platters served at these events with religious invariability. They were impossible to enjoy. The minute I started to eat one, an acquaintance would pop up in front of me, forcing me to swallow the snack in a hurry, just so I could reply to a hello, or plant a kiss with hummus or celery breath on an unsuspecting cheek.

I ran into Jacinta. We had already eyed each other from across the auditorium. She looked sharp, dressed in an executive suit that revealed her attributes without trumpeting them. Several men had already

Roberto Porta-Córdoba

checked her out with awful attempts at concealment. Jacinta didn't harbor sensuality, she emitted it.

"Would you like a cappuccino?" she asked me almost at point blank. When I told her that I'd prefer to have a sandwich at any café in the vicinity, she instead suggested to taste her pasta primavera at home, which –according to what she had confided before- was the best dish she prepared. I thought about it for a moment. I was perfectly aware of the implications, and very much aware of the spurs that a visit to a single woman's home had. I knew that in my position it wasn't the right thing to do. It was simple. Nevertheless, taking advantage that my wife and daughter were out of town, I accepted. I already said I was hungry, but by now, I was also curious.

I feel compelled to warn the reader that the rest of this narration is not pleasant and that it may turn out to be disturbing. What happened to me that night is not an episode that I'd wish upon my worst enemy. It was a cursed encounter. I already made reference to Jacinta's facial expression that rattled me. That night, it would be embedded in my soul for the rest of my life.

We drove to her home in her car. It was a small and sober place, considering Jacinta's robust financial situation, but I thought it was practical and cozy. The clinic connected to the house through a sideway door. In a corner of the bedroom, Jacinta had a small desk with a desktop computer on it, and in front of the bed, a large flat screen TV. I don't see the need to disguise

77

the arousal we both felt as soon as she shut the door. However, we were not ordinary. First, Jacinta fulfilled her promise and cooked a pasta worthy of the most demanding palates. The dinner was magnificent, my appetite was indisputable. We drank lots of wine: Malbec, Merlot, and Pinot Noir. Four or five bottles in total. We indulged in the delight, the gluttony, and the intemperance of two adults believing themselves sovereigns. Two individuals flavoring the froth of arrogance.

We didn't make love. But that doesn't mean I wasn't unfaithful. They say we can sin with our thoughts. I was unfaithful with way more than my thoughts. I was unfaithful with my hands, my lips, and my animal instincts. There were no moral reservations on my part, nor any kind of circumspection on hers. Between the sheets, half-naked, and with my head spinning, I kissed Jacinta's soft fingers, which kept brushing my lips. "Your fingers are lovely", I remember repeating to her, "your fingers are lovely". Jacinta entertained herself sticking her tongue in my ear and biting the lobe with lustful softness. "Your ear is lovely, sugar", she kept whispering, "your ear is lovely".

Almost breathless, I attempted to make her mine once and for all. I fought off the numbness from the wine and heroically managed to hoist my sails, but it was then when she took my face between her hands and gave me the ghastly expression of which I have spoken before. I felt a chill on my cervix and the

Roberto Porta-Córdoba

familiar shiver down my spine. I could only hug her while feeling her naked softness on my chest. Like an inebriated panther, she closed her eyes, and with an ominous grin on her face, she slid down to the bottom of her dreams. I followed suit and also slid into a deep slumber.

A light ray on my face woke me up. It was almost midmorning. I was startled. I had appointments set around noon, but I could barely get up. A throbbing pain in my head knocked me back down on the bed. Jacinta was still sleeping with parted lips and the sheets up to her chin. I detested wine like never before. My lips and my tongue were dried and numb. I was always vulnerable to this ferment's hangover, and at that moment, with my head twirling in a maelstrom of confusion, I got to abhor even the greenest of all grapes.

I finally managed to get up and walk to the bathroom. I needed to splash my face with cold water. The pounding headache felt like a tourniquet in my head. A slight smell of formalin penetrated my nostrils as soon as I opened the door. Then, I saw a jar. The dryness in my throat combined with the shudder I felt almost choked me. Five fingers floated upright inside the jar. They were female fingers. Fingers that I had kissed the night before. Jacinta's fingers!

Shocked and nauseated, I ran out of the bathroom. I found the beautiful surgeon sitting on the bed. She knew what I'd seen inside. "Relax, sugar", she said expectantly, "that's my present to you". Her smile froze my blood and stopped me in my tracks. "Of course, I took my present first", she added, "it would've been hard to take it without my fingers".

I noticed then another jar on the night table next to her. Something yellowish, with red hanging shreds floated inside. Jacinta seemed amused. It was until then that I felt the bandage over my right temple. I gasped in horror when I noticed my right ear was gone. "It's lovely"," she said, looking at the jar, "really lovely. Thank you, sugar."

Roberto Porta-Córdoba

Long Live Da Vinci

Newark International Airport, New Jersey, August 2005. Catherine Erduran, a University of Southern California student, is returning home after a two-week vacation in Europe, which included a stay at her relatives' home in Turkey. Matt Ghanem, a young systems engineer from Tempe, Arizona, is returning home after attending an international conference in Denmark. They met in London while waiting at the gate for their transatlantic flight and resumed their conversation after arrival while transferring their bags to their connecting flights and in the security screening lines.

-I'm going to crash in the plane –Catherine said.

-Why? You didn't sleep in the flight? –Matt asked.

-Not much. I was sandwiched between a man who snored like a bear and a lady who kept going to the bathroom.

-I hear you. It's happened to me…

-To top it off, the person in front of me kept reclining his seat into my knees…

-Typical! –he said.

At the end of the screening line, a security officer signaled Catherine toward a security checkpoint on the left and signaled Matt toward one on the right, but Matt paused and let another passenger pass so he could stay behind Catherine to help her with her carry-on. The officer gave him a cold stare, but didn't say anything.

81

Once they cleared security, they realized that their gates were not that far from each other. Matt offered to walk Catherine to her waiting area before going to his. They shared a liking for TV shows, comedy, and travelling. So far, their conversation had been pleasant.

-I guess I'm early –she said, after noticing few passengers by her gate-. So, please finish telling me about Denmark.

Matt sat next to her and carefully slid his backpack under his seat. He was carrying a crystal souvenir and didn't want to break it on the last leg of the long trip. Likewise, Catherine kept patting the compartment of the bag where she was carrying her new cellphone. She had lost one recently after it fell off from her open purse and now was overcautious about it.

A nearby monitor was playing a documentary about Italian paintings.

-Do you like Italian art? –Matt asked.

-You could say so... not all of it –Catherine said-. And you?

-I only know some of the famous sculptures like the Pieta... David... -Matt said.

-You don't like paintings? –she asked.

-Yeah... I do. I like the Mona Lisa, the Last Supper...

-Oh! You like Da Vinci... -she said with some excitement-. He's my favorite!

-Well... I guess I do –he said, with a compliant smile.

-What? You don't like him much?

-He's okay –he answered.

82

She lowered her head and frowned at him.

-Just okay? –she said, chuckling.

-Well… you know… he was… he is... he was good.

-You don't seem too convinced –she said still frowning, but now also smiling.

-I mean… I like him. I like Da Vinci, but…

-But what? -she said-. You like other painters better?

-I don't know many other painters –he said-. Just Van Gogh, Picasso…

-Do you think they're better than Da Vinci?

-Not really –he said nonchalantly.

Catherine chuckled softly and patted the cellphone inside the bag. Matt looked at her with amusement.

-You have to admit he's the best, come on! – she said.

Matt looked at the floor and smiled.

-I love him –she said-. To me, he was a genius.

Matt arched his eyebrows and kept quiet.

-He had so many talents –she continued-. He painted… he sculptured… he designed… he invented things…

A stubby man sat in front of them. He was wearing a blue windbreaker that bore the word Italy across the front in white letters and the Italian flag on a sleeve. He took a quick glimpse at them.

-I don't know –Matt said.

-You don't know, what? –she chuckled softly.

-I think…

-What? –she asked.

-I don't know. I just think the guy is overrated.

83

Catherine's eyes opened wide. She cupped her mouth with her hand. Then she glanced to the stubby man and chuckled again. Matt chuckled, too.

-What do you mean overrated? –she asked with disbelief.

-I mean... I don't know... the guy was good, but... I don't think he was a genius.

-You don't think so?

-Honestly... no.

-But... he did all those things... he designed a flying machine... a tank... he drew accurate maps...

-Yeah... that's true, but...

-Do you really think he's overrated? –asked Catherine, attempting a serious face.

-Well... let's put it this way. To me, a real genius would be Franklin.

-Franklin?

-Yes. Benjamin Franklin.

-What do you mean? –She asked with curiosity-. He wasn't an artist.

-I know he wasn't an artist, but we're talking about geniuses... as a whole... right?

Catherine conceded.

-Don't get me wrong. I respect Da Vinci – continued Matt-. But, I prefer Franklin.

-I like Benjamin Franklin, too –Catherine said-. But, why do you think he was better than Da Vinci?

-I didn't say he was better. I said that I prefer him.

-Ok, but... why? –she asked, looking at the stubby man out of the corner of her eye.

-Well... if you think about it, Da Vinci was into too many things at the same time.

84

Roberto Porta-Córdoba

-Yeah, but so was Franklin.

-You're right, but there's a difference.

-And... may I know what that difference is? – asked Catherine with an inquisitive smile.

Matt leaned a little towards her, as if about to share a secret. Catherine listened attentively.

-Franklin finished what he started –he said-. Da Vinci left many things incomplete.

Catherine put a serious face on. Matt continued.

-Da Vinci had great ideas... but he wasn't focused... he kept hopping from one project to another... -he said.

-That's not true! –Catherine said, containing her laughter with one hand.

An airport attendant rolled a man in a wheelchair and left him near them. The man thanked the attendant and smiled at Catherine. Matt went on.

-He left many sketches... blueprints... a lot of unfinished things, and sometimes he seemed to be in a rush... -he said.

-What do you mean he seemed to be in a rush?

-Well... he messed it up when he painted the Last Supper.

-You're mad! –She said with disbelief while glancing in the direction of the stubby man-. I watched a documentary and it took him three long years to paint it!

-I don't know –Matt said, smiling-. But he surely rushed his choice of materials.

-How do you know that?

-Because the painting began deteriorating only a few years after he finished it.

-Aw, come on! You sound as if you just read that somewhere –she chuckled-. I'm sure Franklin made some mistakes, too!

-Maybe –he replied-. But at least he invented practical things, like bifocal lenses… swimming fins… the lighting rod… street lamps…

Catherine looked away with a sneer, tapping again the cellphone inside her bag.

-As if it was not enough, he was one of the Founding Fathers, a successful diplomat, and even found time to write almanacs –Matt continued-. Da Vinci got nothing on him!

Catherine rolled he eyes and pretended to get upset. He pointed a finger to Matt.

-Leave Da Vinci alone or I won't talk to you anymore –she whispered with a smile.

-Ok, fine! –Matt said, playfully closing his eyes-. Long live Da Vinci! Long live Da Vinci!

It was then when the stubby man in the blue windbreaker got up, jumped on Matt, and threw him to the floor, while the man in the wheelchair jumped from it and did the same to a horrified Catherine. With dazzling speed, and amid people's screams, a dozen of undercover agents and uniformed guards appeared and started shouting and pointing their guns to the subdued couple laying on the carpet.

As airport security and police cordoned the area off and directed nearby passengers to other gates, trained dogs and heavily armed guards swarmed the scene. Catherine and Matt were yanked from the floor. They had no idea what was happening and couldn't muster a word. They were both shaking with fear as their hands were handcuffed behind their backs.

86

It took less than twenty minutes for the airport authorities to realize their blunder, and then less than five minutes for all security guards, undercover agents, policemen and dogs to disappear from the scene. Catherine and Matt had been the subjects of identity mistake. For several months, the Interpol had been following the tracks of a terrorist cell in Europe believed to be planning a hijack or a bombing in U.S. soil. An alert had been issue that week on several flights departing from London and the airport security in Newark had wrongly profiled the pair upon arrival.

Once under surveillance, they made matters worse when Matt sat by the "wrong" gate and Catherine kept nervously tapping something in her bag. And of course, it didn't help that Matt kept saying "Da Vinci", unaware that it was the codename of the suspected cell leader.

Roberto Porta-Córdoba

Diana the Unfortunate

I was feeling good today. Unlike yesterday, or Tuesday last week, when my soul ached. Why did my soul ache? Why would I suffer any kind of pain? I didn't know. I only knew it was to time to hit the road. The daily obligations awaited in the outskirts of my mind.

I had not even walked three blocks when her sweet and affectional voice arrived.

-You're unbelievable... it's not even seven in the morning and you're on your way –she said.

-Hi Diana! How are you? You're also early! –I said, planting a kiss on her cheek.

Diana. Graphic designer. Born with an abnormal forward curve in the upper spine, a hunchback. Poor woman. As for me, I was feeling good today. As for me, I was happy.

-Your business trip –she said- are you all set?

-Of course! –I lied.

-Great! You deserve it. You work so hard for that company.

Of course I deserved it. I absolutely deserved it. I probably deserved it. I think I deserved it. Did I deserve it?

-And... the office? Is everything fine at the office? –she asked.

-Sure! Everything is fine at the office – I lied again.

-I'm glad to hear it –she said- you're really a lucky person.

It was a sunny day. The weather was gorgeous. I had to be smiling, right? I had to feel like laughing, right? I had to unleash my imagination and envision the white and shiny clouds forming a cotton throne for me. I had to assume that the clear blue of the sky was my reward for starting a grand new day. I agree, I agree… I got it.

Diana and I walked across Trovadores, that wide, long and noisy avenue, always full of people, always full of smells, always full of warmth. Diana started telling me something about her job. I listened to her. I'm proud of that. I'm proud that I can listen to whoever talks to me. I have always been polite. I have also been proud of that. Of course I am polite! Why wouldn't I? Her conversation was captivating. Her mindset was unique. Her perspective on everything that seemed gray was colorful. An exemplary woman of great sensitivity. We crossed another avenue. We walked by the market and the butchers. The sidewalks were full, our pace became slower. The smell was unpleasant. There was a stench of shellfish and rotten sea food. Diana and I walked in silence with our noses feeling ashamed. Minutes later, we resumed our talk.

-Do you have plans for this Friday? –she asked.

I knew I had no plans, but I adopted a thoughtful expression, I frowned, and I looked up and to the right, as if trying to remember something.

-Mmmm… I don't think so- I replied.

-Good! –Diana smiled, while sidestepping a small puddle on the sidewalk- I'd like to invite you and your wife to a party.

-A party?

90

Roberto Porta-Córdoba

-Yes! At my house. It's a surprise birthday party for a coworker. There will be some friends, we'll have some snacks, music, beer… oh! But, no smoking! I can't have that smell at home. You haven't gone back to smoking, have you?

-Of course, not! –I lied-. It's been three years since I quit.

-So, what do you say?

-Well…

-You'll have a chance to try my Thai basil chicken. It's delicious!

-I…

-Are you coming?

-Er…

-Come on! I haven't seen your wife in a while.

I couldn't decline her invitation. On the street, the cars and buses heated the asphalt recklessly, making the air smelled of burned rubber. My briefcase hung from my left shoulder. It was heavy. It was full of documents, clogged with papers, packed with deadlines, filled with urgencies, stuffed with angst.

-I saw your brother last week. He looked good... and his children! –she said raising her voice and startling me a bit- they're so beautiful! My God! Those kids!

-Yes, they are cute–I said.

-And… what about you? Are you ready for that step? –she said, laughing- Cristina seems to be good with kids. You'll have to share the news as soon as it happens! –she said bursting in a laughter that startled me again. My heart beat at the speed of dreadfulness.

-Of course, we'll share the news – I said.

91

Fictions of an Immigrant

One more block separated us from the subway station. From there to my office, it would probably take me 15 more minutes. I would be on time. I practiced punctuality. I was proud to be always on time. I had always been on time… besides, I was feeling good today. Why wouldn't I?

I needed to finish a very important project. It was a tough project, full of details and numbers. It was a demanding project, a challenging, complex, difficult, and rugged project. I didn't know at what time I would finish it. I had no idea at what time I would get off work. The project was really daring, just like my boss had predicted. I look forward to the project with impatience. I was ready for it. I wanted to dive into it. That's what my boss had suggested. He was always right. I was feeling good, my friends. I was pleased. My boss was such a smart man. I was feeling great.

-I'm sleepy. I don't feel like working today – Diana said.

-How come?

-I went to bed almost at midnight. I was babysitting three children.

-Gosh! Whose children?

-A friend's children. She went to college with me.

-Did they behave?

-Not really. The boys fell asleep early, but the little girl was unstoppable. My God! She wouldn't even let me watch TV. She had me telling her stories for over two hours! But… she's so sweet!

-You really like kids –I said.

We arrived to the station. A hurried man bumped into me. He paused and apologized. I smiled.

92

Diana smiled. The man smiled. He went on his way. We went on ours. Diana said something. I didn't pay attention. I felt my face burning. I was thinking of the man. I felt like following him. I felt like pulling him by his shirt and breaking his face, fracturing his nose, grabbing him by the throat. I felt like... strangling him.

-Well, my friend, it was nice to see you –Diana said as we reached the subway entrance-. Don't forget Friday's party. I'll call you at work to remind you. Give my regards to Cristina. Have a good day!

-Thank you, Diana. You, too. –I said.

With her charming smile, she resumed her stride. She stopped to greet someone at a newspaper stand.

I lit up a cigarette before descending the stairs. I hadn't quit smoking. How could I attend that party? My wife didn't talk to me. She hadn't done so since I pushed her away at a family gathering. It wasn't the first time. My brother chided me for that. He was angry at me. He and his wife loved her. My wife feared me. She didn't want to see me anymore. I was informed she was filing for divorce.

My trip? Please don't make me laugh. There was no trip. The company cancelled it. I didn't meet my sales goal for the year, once again. Who would've thought? Our sales were so high! What a pity. I'll try harder next year. I'll do my best. My boss was right. My boss is very smart.

I watched Diana say goodbye to her acquaintance. She was laughing. She looked amused. The sidewalk was getting crowded by the minute. It was getting warmer. I smelled a distant scent of ham and eggs. Finally, I lost sight of Diana. She walked

93

away with that big hump on her back. Poor Diana, poor my friend. That ugly hump ... that misshapen hump. I felt sad for her. Born with that hunchback on her back. How bad she must feel. Poor Diana, poor my friend. How unfortunate she was.

Roberto Porta-Córdoba

My Coincidence

I always enjoyed reading about coincidences. I liked reading about what the dictionary defined as "a remarkable concurrence of events or circumstances without apparent causal connection." When I was in middle school, I had a shoebox with newspaper and magazine clippings about coincidences. Then, in high school, I moved them to a couple of scrapbooks and I kept adding more clippings. Later, in college, the internet advent allowed me to access so much information that I was able to set up a website about the topic. My last endeavor was to create a YouTube channel dedicated to my old hobby, although I have to admit that I no longer dedicate much time to it.

Among the gems of my early collection I remember having some classic ones like Mark Twain being born in 1835, a year Halley's Comet appeared, and passing away in 1910, the year of the comet's next appearance, something the writer even predicted. Another well-known coincidence I filed under American writers was the one about Edgar Allan Poe and the only novel he ever wrote: "The Narrative of Arthur Gordon Pym of Nantucket," in which one of the characters, a cabin boy in a damaged boat adrift in high sea, is eaten by the other three hungry and desperate survivors after drawing lots to determine the victim. The name of the cannibalized character was Richard Parker, and the novel was published in 1838. Fate had it that 46 years later a real tragedy occurred in a

95

damaged English sailboat off the coast of South Africa, in which a crew of four, crazed by hunger and the ingesting of sea water, had to raffle the death and cannibalization of one of them to survive. The unlucky victim was also a cabin boy, and his name was Richard Parker.

One of my favorite coincidences as a child, was that of King Umberto I of Italy. I remember my poor parents having to hear it from me at least twice a week, during breakfast or dinner time, not to mention family reunions, birthdays and anniversaries. On the night of July 28, 1900, King Umberto I was having dinner with an attendant at a restaurant in Monza when he noticed that the owner of the establishment was identical to him in body and face. Amused, the king invited him to his table to talk and both discovered even more similarities: the restaurant's owner was also named Umberto; both had been born in Turin on the same date; and the two had married girls named Margherita, also on the same date. Finally, they discovered that the owner had opened the restaurant on the very same day of the king's crowning. Impressed with so many coincidences, the monarch invited his double to accompany him to an athletic competition he had to attend the next day. Unfortunately, once in the stadium, the king's aide informed him that the owner of the restaurant had been killed by gunshots that morning. Incredibly, as the king expressed his regret, an anarchist emerged from the crowd and shot him, killing him on the spot.

96

In my teenage years, I always hoped to meet my double or to experience a great coincidence. Naively, I would always try to find coincidences where there were none and kept reading my magazines and clippings with the same enthusiasm of the first time. Unluckily for me, I never experienced a real coincidence. I remember reaching my high school senior year still keeping a subliminal hope, and while I no longer bored my friends or family with my obsession, I continued watching documentaries or news on TV related to the subject.

One of the last coincidences I remember adding to the collection was the one involving the famous British actor Sir Anthony Hopkins, the same one who mesmerized us in his Oscar-winning role as Hannibal Lecter in the early 90s. The amazing coincidence took place around 1972, way before Hopkins reached the superstardom and prestige that included being knighted by the Queen. Hopkins had just landed a leading role in the film "The Girl from Petrovka" based on a book written by George Feifer. To prepare for his role, Hopkins tried to buy the book at several bookstores in London, but none had it available. While he waited for his train back home at the subway station, he noticed a book apparently discarded on the bench. He couldn't believe his eyes when he realized it was "The Girl from Petrovka." But the story doesn't end there. Two years later, in the middle of filming, author George Feifer visited the shooting location and got to meet Hopkins. Feifer saw the actor with the book and joked

97

that he didn't have a copy of his own. He said that he had lent the last one, containing his own written notes, to a friend who had lost it somewhere in London. Astonished, Hopkins showed Feifer the book he had found. It had the notes scribbled in the margins. It was the same book!

I added a few other coincidences to the collection, but that was the one I recall the most today, maybe because of my fondness for books and movies. Around that time, already out of college, I had ended my quest to live my own coincidence. I had settled for one that involved the last name of my first college roommate and the last name of my first co-teacher. They were both McLaughlin, and they were both engraved next to my last name on similar door name plates, first on the dorm door in my first semester in college, and years later on the classroom door at the first school I worked for. To be honest, I wasn't impressed with my coincidence. It was a nice one, but I didn't find so thrilling. However, already consumed by other interests and responsibilities, I assumed that it was the coincidence destiny had in store for me and I retired my old hobby. Little did I know how wrong I was.

Five years later, a new teaching post took me and my family to another state. I had been married for 8 years and we had been blessed with twins, twice. Although my wife worked in retail management and I had finished a graduate degree in night school, we both worked hard to make ends meet and sometimes felt

98

overwhelmed and exhausted. Our jobs seemed stable and family life was good, but there were stretches when it seemed we were financially stuck. We weren't saving much, our budget kept shrinking, and our kids were growing fast. Unbeknown to me, just like my children's mother had delivered them in coincidental fashion, fate was ready to deliver to us the mother of all coincidences.

It all began with an in-service training all teachers had to attend as the start of the school year. I wasn't too excited about it because the workshop location was downtown and traffic was always a pain in that area. To make matters worse, the teacher I carpooled with had to leave midmorning because of a family emergency, inadvertently taking my lunch bag with him. However, the training was very interesting and I found it very useful. Not such a bad day, after all. Around 3 pm, munching on my third bag of chips, I called an Uber to take me home.

The first thing I noticed when I got in the back seat of the Uber was a worn out book in a net behind the driver's seat. I pulled it out and looked at the title. It was a paperback edition of a novel which by chance I had been wanting to read for a while. The book's glossy cover was cracked, and although the pages were still tight, the first pages of the book looked yellowish and soft, while the back fore edge looked white and almost in mint condition. Somehow, the book seemed familiar. When I opened it and started browsing the first pages, I started to remember that I had read it, at

99

least partially. Then, it hit me. I had purchased this novel months before. That was the reason it looked familiar! What I noticed next left me aghast. There, on the wrinkled first page of the book was a faded, almost indiscernible scribble of a signature. It was my signature!

At the next traffic light, I wanted to show the book to the driver and ask him about it, but I held back because he was busy entering something on his phone's GPA. By then, I was positive it was the very same book I had started to read before I lost it somewhere. I couldn't hold back a chuckle. What were the odds? When I finally asked the driver, he told me that some passenger had left it there months ago, and that he'd decided to keep it in the car because most passengers entertained themselves with it and, besides, he didn't like reading.

I was in awe. I started to remember having used an Uber the last time my car was in the shop, almost a year ago. I also recalled my wife nagging me for having lost a book the first week I had bought it. I wanted to tell the driver it was my book, showed him my signature, and keep it, but, would he believe me? Maybe he'd think I was just a weirdo trying to steal the book. The signature was faded and didn't exactly resembled the one on my driver's license or on my teacher's ID. The situation felt awkward.

Eventually, as we neared my home, and sounding cringe, I told him about the coincidence and offered to buy the book from him. He gave me a

Roberto Porta-Córdoba

puzzled look. Maybe he would've just let me keep it if I asked him, but I had already taken my wallet out. I was decided to get the book no matter what. It almost looked like an assault. By chance, my wife and one of our kids were checking the mailbox when the Uber stopped in front of our townhouse. She saw me handling a $20 bill to the driver, the only bill I had in my wallet at that moment. The driver gave me a startled look as he pocketed the bill and told me to keep the beat-up book. He surely thought I was a wacko or an idiot.

Needless to say, my wife wasn't happy with my impulsive spending. At first, she thought I was tipping the driver, but she wasn't impressed when I told her the whole story. She rightfully felt that I had paid more for a worn out, dirty book, than what I would've paid for a new one. My excitement did nothing to appease her. To her, my old hobby was a thing of the past and she found it silly that I spent money on something like that. She rolled her eyes and smiled sardonically during dinner when I later shared the story with the children.

For the next three days, I shared my coincidence with everyone at work. I couldn't believe it! It transported me back to my childhood when I harassed my parents and everybody else with my repetitive obnoxious stories. After years of not logging into the abandoned website and YouTube channel, I felt compelled to go and update "my coincidence" entry. Chancing upon the very same Uber I had ridden

101

months before in a suburban area of millions, and still finding the same book I had left inside, had to be a more remarkable concurrence of events than the matching name plates I had held so far as the pinnacle of my personal coincidences. I even compared it to the famous book Sir Anthony Hopkins had found in the subway station. I finally had a truly huge coincidence to brag about!

But fate wasn't done playing its capricious game. When I said earlier that fate was ready to deliver the mother of all coincidences, I actually should've said that fate was ready to deliver the "grandmother" of all coincidences. Nothing could've prepared me for what was coming.

Once my initial exhilaration had worn off, I decided to give the fateful book a read. After all, I had bought it because I had read good reviews about it. One night, while my wife worked late on her laptop, I sat on the bed next to her and began flipping the yellowish fusty first pages. I couldn't help thinking how many Uber riders must have browsed the book, day after day, week after week, month after month. Following my wife's advice, I cleaned it up with a damp cloth. It still seemed funny to me that more than half of the fore edge looked brand new, because the Uber passengers only had time to read or browse through the first pages. To check the condition of the book's binding, I flipped the back pages hard to test its firmness, and then I saw it: a mint Mega Millions ticket tucked inside the book's back pages.

102

When I showed it to my wife, she thought I was kidding. We hadn't bought lotto tickets in years. We quickly assumed that some clueless Uber rider must have left it there. But, why would a passenger do that in a book that is not his? Was there a name or anything written on the ticket? I checked, but nothing was written. The ticket looked brand new. However, when I checked the date of purchase I noticed it had been bought almost a year to the date. I made an effort to remember exactly when I had taken the car to the mechanic and I suddenly realized it had been almost a year. Then, it came to me. I hate carrying coins in my pockets and I remembered getting rid of them by buying a lotto ticket at the shop, before calling my Uber. How could a lotto ticket go unnoticed for so long to so many people?

My wife shook her head and chuckled. It was clearly expired. We knew lotto tickets were forfeited if not claimed in about six months. Just out of curiosity, I grabbed my smartphone from the night table to do some research. The Mega Millions website said that expiration dates depended on the state where tickets were bought. In our state, the time period for claiming a prize was one year from the draw date. The ticket was still valid, it would expire in 3 days. Impulsively, I scrolled down to the past winning numbers section displaying on the screen and clicked on the ticket's draw date. Then, I compared the six numbers. To my astonishment… they all matched! My eyeballs almost came out when I saw the jackpot: 245 million dollars!

My wife couldn't hear my yelling when I told her. She had her headphones on and her eyes glued on the laptop.

It took the quick arrival of our frightened children to our bedroom and the angry pursue of my wife around the room to stop my insane up-and-down jumping and screaming. The kids thought I had gone crazy. I was so charged up that I didn't even notice when I hit the fan lamp and cut the top of my head. There was glass and blood on the rug, the sheets, and all over my pajamas. I felt like in a daze. It was until my wife literally dragged me inside the bathroom that I was able to catch my breath. Understandably, she was distraught. The older twins called 911. By the time an ambulance arrived, I had already shared the incredible news with my wife. It took me a while to convince her to verify it on her laptop. She also thought I had gone nuts. When we left to the hospital, she had calmly placed the ticket in a safe place; the younger twins came with us; and the older ones stayed behind cleaning the mess.

My wife wrote her resignation letter a couple of days after claiming the prize. I arranged with the school to finish the first quarter, citing personal reasons. We were able to hide our identities, despite the media scrutiny caused by the large jackpot amount combined with the growing mystery created by our unintentional delay to claim it.

As for the book, it sits now in a plexiglass display case in our Colorado winter house. I never

Roberto Porta-Córdoba

went back to finishing it, but I did go back to revising my coincidence website for the second time in a short while. I have a strong feeling there will be no more revisions for now.

Roberto Porta-Córdoba

Icarus

My brother was laid off from his job of nineteen years. Months later, he lost his life savings when the market crashed. I respectfully beg you to believe me when I say that I didn't want to watch the video.

I expected a somewhat older fellow when Jeremy picked me up at the airport. He did not come alone. He brought along his four-year old son, a very lively and sweet boy.

"So, this is your first time in Frisco," said Jeremy.

"Yes, it is," I admitted. "My brother always invited me to come over... every Thanksgiving, every Christmas... every Memorial Day. Never made it, though."

Indeed, every time I intended to visit San Francisco something turned up. Whether it was the cancellation of a business meeting in the area, or a social event that my wife deemed impossible to call off, getting to know this city -reputed by its cosmopolitanism, eclecticism, and liberal boldness- was always a dead end for me.

Jeremy's family proved very hospitable and kind. His wife Sofia and two sons welcomed me as if I were an old acquaintance. They lived in Daly City. He worked at an insurance company and she managed a fast-food eatery. I could tell that -although not deprived- they worked very hard to make it.

I subtly turned down Jeremy's offer to stay at their home. I checked into a nearby hotel. Although my

107

stay would be short, I didn't want to cause them an unnecessary burden. They had already done a lot by playing host to a stranger. For all practical purposes, that's what I was to them.

Over the weekend, I declined to watch the video. First, I wanted to get a feel of the area. Jeremy showed me around. No need to bore anyone with the details. If anyone is familiar with San Francisco, they will remember Lombard Street, Fisherman Wharf, the fog, the coldest summers around, and so on. If someone is not familiar, trying to describe this beautiful city would be a futile exercise and a sinful waste of time. I would prefer that they just go.

I visited the Golden Gate Bridge, of course. I saw it. I walked it. I felt it. Before doing so, I was intrigued as to why this bridge –with its attractive international orange color- was the favorite place in the world to commit suicide. After crossing it by foot escorted by Sofia –Jeremy refused to come-, I thought I understood. The view of the bay and the city skyline were gorgeous, but were also terminal. The deck of the bridge is 245 feet above the water, and anyone falling over is sure to impact the surface at approximately 80 miles per hour; an almost certain death. Only 2% of all jumpers have survived in the past.

But maybe what appeals most to suicide candidates is the bridge's low railing. With little effort, anyone can climb and jump over because the bridge is one of the few landmarks around the world without a safety barrier. Sofia told me the city has been trying to install some kind of suicide barrier for several years now, but that aesthetics and financing had ironically become the real barrier.

108

"Money is a barrier that works," I said. "A really sad barrier."

I was appalled when I read that an average of 20 people kill themselves at the bridge every year. And I almost came to tears when I read some of the stories: people in debt, misunderstood teenagers, bipolar fellows, alienated adults, or people with terminal illnesses. All jumping to their death to simply go under the rug. Is there so much sorrow in this land to encourage a person to actually make that jump? It takes a lot of guts to make that move. After looking down at the cold water, I didn't even want to come close to the railing. I got dizzy in a second. What goes through the mind of a suicidal person right at that moment? Doesn't anyone really care? I suppose many of us do… but only after they made the jump.

Before watching the video, Jeremy showed me a painting he downloaded from the web. It was titled "Landscape with the Fall of Icarus". It shows the mythological Icarus splashing against the water after the wax of his feathers melted because of the sun. Amid the vastness of the landscape, the splash is hardly noticeable.

"It's just like the jumpers," said my host, "there's a quick splash when they complete their fall. Then… no trace. Life goes on."

Sofia sent the kids to bed. She served coffee. Jeremy pressed the play button. My eyes focused on the TV screen. In the video, Sofia and the boys wave at the camera from the Golden Gate Bridge. There are no pedestrians around. The three of them are close to the bridge railing. Jeremy says something, but the wind makes it inaudible. And then, my brother appears in

109

the background. I swallow hard. The kids continue waving as they slowly approach the camera. My brother is about 40 feet away, looking down. Sofia smiles and Jeremy continues recording. Then, with the cups of coffee in our hands, we see when my brother climbs the railing, crosses himself, and jumps to his death. He must have made a splash, like Icarus.

Roberto Porta-Córdoba

Ghost Travelers

I met Nikola during one of my trips abroad. I traveled to multiple locations in Europe as part of my job as a financial consultant. Madrid was one of my frequent stops, a city I really enjoyed visiting. I considered its airport one of the most comfortable and accessible of the continent, a sort of testament to the improvement of Spain's economy in the last two decades.

Maybe that improvement was what attracted Nikola from his native Bulgaria years ago. He confided me that business was good at first in Spain, but then things got sour for him. He wouldn't elaborate what kind of business he was in. I never had time to ask him. Or maybe I kept forgetting.

Nikola was a ghost traveler, one of those less fortunate people who lost his job, so badly that it'd made him also lose his trust in society and his confidence in finding another one. Instead. Like 20 other homeless people, he lived in the Madrid-Barajas International Airport, the second largest airport in Europe.

They're called ghost travelers because they all look like travelers: they carry a bag or pull a piece of luggage or a carryon. They seem in a hurry, sometimes with a newspaper under an arm, looking up the flight departure boards, looking down at an old boarding pass, walking intently toward their flight. Except, they have no flight to catch.

Ghost travelers don't beg for money, they don't threaten passengers, and don't attempt to rob anyone.

111

Fictions of an Immigrant

They just pretend to be tourist or businessmen who just lost their passport, their documentation, or their wallet. They come from different places: Turkey, Greece, Croatia, and from some remote ones like Korea and Mozambique.

That's how I saw Nikola the first time. He stood next to my line when I was checking in, looking puzzled and anguished, reaching for his pockets, searching for something. "What's going on?" I remember asking him while other passengers looked over. "I just lost my bag with my passport and wallet, I need to call my embassy... I can't believe it!" he replied.

Most people turn away when ghost travelers do their show. Skepticism is automatic. However, some good souls -or gullible people like me- want to help and end up hearing the whole 5-minute story of how they must catch the next flight or else his job, family, or whatever would suffer the consequences.

I gave Nikola 10 euros the first time. I really felt bad for his situation. Anyone who has lost a wallet, a purse, or an ID in a public place, knows what kind of downer that is. Nikola looked and sounded distressed. He thanked me and quickly walked away. I had no time to even ask for his name. Little did I know that with my contribution Nikola had already surpassed his daily quota of 40 euros and he was as happy as a clam.

Like most ghost travelers, Nikola aimed at collecting enough cash to buy some food and possibly rent a room in a hostel at Barajas, the nearest town to the airport. They walk an average of 12 miles around the airport every day, hopping from terminal to another while trying to pass undetected by making fictitious

112

phone calls, quickly going in and out of the restrooms, and striking casual conversation with anyone near them when they feel observed.

That's unnecessary, though. After a couple of weeks, security guards and airport personnel get to know most of them. They can identify them by their odd demeanor and the cloth they wear. The guards consider them harmless, and since the five terminals are considered public places, there's no impending need to permanently remove them from the premises. Like an airlines agent once told me: "They have become part of the scenery, they blend with the walls. They have become invisible." With around 150,000 people walking through the airport daily, I didn't find it difficult to believe.

Nikola's case was in no way similar to the one of the Iranian who lived for 18 years in Charles de Gaulle Airport in Paris, and even inspired a movie starring Tom Hanks. In that case, the French offered residency to the man, but he opted for staying inside the terminal. Nikolas never received an offer of residency from Spain because he already had it. He just wanted a job, a job without a boss, a job somewhere in a beautiful place.

The second time I saw him, he offered his help at the counter when my luggage exceeded the weight limit. I don't know how he knew, but Nikola was ready with a big bag from a Madrid store and quickly helped me transfer some of my belongings to it. I tipped him with 5 euros and became curious when I recognized him from the public "ordeal" he'd suffered two weeks before. "I know you," I said, "what are you still doing here?"

113

Nikola eagerly told me his story at one of the fast food kiosks nearby. I invited him for coffee, but he ordered a glass of wine. It became obvious he was an indigent. A very clever one, indeed. What I didn't know was the extent of his homelessness and the skills he applied to survive his routine. By the end of his first glass -which he drank slowly, staring at the wine, savoring each drop- I learned that Nikola had been living in the airport for almost 6 years. I was in disbelief.

After the second glass, he had described to me his typical day at the airport: waking up at 5 in the morning after sleeping in a corner or on a cushioned seat, like many real travelers do; washing his face and armpits in the restroom; brushing his teeth and making sure his shirt was not too wrinkled. When he could afford it, his morning ritual began with a warm bath at a Barajas hostel and some laundry.

After the freshening routine came breakfast time -most shops' workers knew him and offered him coffee or croissants- , and finally worktime: posing as the desperate traveler who lost his documentation, serving as a guide, as a translator -Nikola spoke Bulgarian, Russian, English, Spanish, and French-, or simply helping people in need of plastic wrapping to secure their luggage, after seizing a leftover roll from one of the airport businesses.

Nikola had finished a third glass of wine by the time he filled me in on how his days at the airport were always the same. No weekends, no holidays, no specialties, except for the season changes, when daylight and temperature would slightly alter his routine and some of the ghost travelers would end up

114

Roberto Porta-Córdoba

leaving. "I talk to most of the others... they're nice folks, especially Manny, the Venezuelan. I talk to him all the time... but, each of us has a business to take care of... sometimes we don't have time to talk much... they prefer to connect their tablets or phones to the restaurants wi-fi and read the news," Nikolas told me.

Before I left for my gate, I asked him how I could help him. I asked about his family, relatives, or friends. He said he was divorced with no kids and that he'd never gotten serious with any woman in Spain, but he added that he "would like to get back to normal life one day" and that the best help I could give him was to land him a job in Sweden or Finland. "Never in Spain, nor in Bulgaria," he pointed out.

I didn't see Nikola for two months, despite looking for him during my stopovers or work visits to Madrid. Nevertheless, I always remembered his request and had it at the back of my mind. He'd told me he was great at sales and marketing, and I totally believed him.

When I got to see him again, it was winter, and I almost didn't recognize him under two thick hooded sweaters and an old scarf. "I need to stay warm," he said, "transit between terminals on the buses is a killer some days!" I gave him some cash, a scarf, and snacks. I also told him that there was a possibility for a job, not in Sweden or Finland, but in nearby Denmark. "Great!" he replied, "that's close enough."

Luckily, I had some business acquaintances in that country and a few weeks after that conversation, I was able to set up a Skype interview for him with a recruiter. I lent him an old tablet and made sure he had

115

enough identification documents on him, even if expired. I tried to arrange for the process to be completed during a 4-day work stay in Spain. It worked out fine. On my way home, I met Nikola at the airport and he told me how the interview had gone well and how thankful he was for my help.

A few days later, I received a copy of the e-mail the company sent to him. He was hired as a full-time translator! I immediately contacted Nikola through a mobile phone I had activated for him; I told him I would be in Spain in a couple of days, and that I would like to personally give him his train or plane ticket to Denmark. Nikola sounded happy, although a little skeptical. A formal job after 6 years! My wife opened a champagne bottle to celebrate. She was also rooting for Nikola. We were happy for him.

Things had worked out beautifully and the big day arrived. It had taken a while, but there we were, in opposite situations: Nikola -all dressed up and shaved- ready to board a flight, and I, ready to stay on the ground and do some work. This time I escorted him to his gate. Funny how we had switched roles! He was smiling, but he looked nervous and restless. I told him he would be fine, that he was a smart man with a good soul, and that I would certainly see him in the near future when a business trip took me to Denmark.

A couple of airport workers who had known him all this time joined me in hugging him and wishing him well before he boarded his plane. He waved and smiled timidly as he disappeared into the jet bridge. I couldn't help noticing another ghost traveler watching from a discreet distance, as if saying goodbye to an old friend. Nikola had introduced me to him

116

months before. Before I could approach him, he had already vanished. He had to get busy. Time was money at the airport.

I was feeling well. I felt I had done the best to help somebody, which had not been one of my traits in life. For the first time in years, I felt less selfish and more accomplished. I decided to celebrate with a nice sangria glass and sat at one of the fancy bars that make modern airports look like a main street. Soon, I had to get back my hotel and start planning my work routine. Somehow, since meeting Nikola, I had learned to appreciate my job more, with its highs and lows.

About twenty minutes later, I paid the check and walked out of the bar. I didn't notice anything unusual at first. The Madrid airport was busy and noisy all the time. However, when I saw airport personnel, security guards, and policemen running from different directions, I knew something was going on.

I hesitated for a moment before walking in the direction of the metro station. I'm a curious person by nature and when I saw how a commotion was slowly forming with people walking fast and alarmed, I asked an airport agent what was happening. She told me two of the terminals had just been shut down because of an upcoming emergency landing. She wasn't sure about the details, but one of her peers added that it could even be a case of terrorism. They both looked confused and alarmed.

It took me only five minutes to make it to the next train. When I heard the word terrorism, I knew I didn't want anything to do with it. I hurried to the hotel a bit startled and anxious to hear the news. I just wanted to be as far as possible from the airport. Back

117

in my room, I flipped through the local channels which were already broadcasting the situation, although there were contradictions on what was taking place.

I left the TV on and the bathroom door open while I took a shower and prepare for an evening meeting. My curiosity was rewarded when I heard the confirmed news: an airplane bound for Denmark had to return abruptly to the Madrid airport when a passenger became distressed and started yelling and hitting the windows. He demanded to return to the ground while yelling "I don't want to go! I don't want to go!"

The crew had been able to contain his aggressive behavior with the help of some passengers, but the captain had no choice but to return to the airport immediately. First reports informed that although most passengers remained calm, several were hysterical and terrified. Fortunately, the plane landed safely and the personnel at the airport reacted swiftly and professionally. The flights schedule, however, was a mess, with many of them postponed or cancelled.

I sat on my bed in disbelief when I noticed who the unruly passenger was. Nikola's mugshot was all over the news! Every channel in Spain was showing the scenes at the airport, with a handcuffed Nikola being taken into custody, charged with countless safety violations.

I attempted to visit him in jail the following day, but he refused to see me. In fact, I never saw him again in person. Just on the TV news, where he was mentioned for several days before slipping in oblivion once again.

118

What exactly happened to Nikola? Why did he change his mind after accepting his new promising job? What made him abort a seemingly great opportunity to get back the normal life he wanted? I figured his soul was not ready to exchange a lead role in a cage for a submissive position in freedom. Maybe he trembled at the thought of losing a precarious stability in order to get a taste of uncertainty.

Whatever the case, I guess I'll never know. Nikola was banned from all Spanish airports and public transportation places after being released 36 months later. The local authorities lost track of him and the new generation of ghost travelers don't have time to remember him.

Fictions of an Immigrant

Roberto Porta-Córdoba

Nastaran's Screams

Nastaran was seven years old when she saw her first horror movie. It was by accident. Her older sister and her parents didn't notice she'd sneaked out of bed and into the living room. They realized until they turned their heads away from the TV screen startled by a scary scene and saw her standing behind the couch. Nastaran didn't flinch. She showed no emotion as she stared at the screen. When they asked her why she wasn't scared, she said, "Because it's a movie set, and in front of that zombie there are several cameras, a director, people holding microphones, and more people holding lights and stuff. It's not real."

Not only was Nastaran logical and fearless since an early age, she was also an advocate of fairness. She felt she was missing out on something every time she saw her friends bite her nails and screamed with fear at the scary movies, or when she yawned at fiction books that were supposed to be frightening or dreadful, or when she watched documentaries about people experiencing paranormal activities. She wanted to be scared, she wanted to know how it felt to be spooked, she wanted to see a ghost, she wanted to experience the paranormal, but her reality hyperawareness wouldn't allow it. "It's not fair!" she would complain.

Nastaran was confident and resolute. When she approached her 10th birthday, her parents asked her how she wanted to celebrate the occasion. She

121

requested a butter cake with a piece missing, but with the sides of the missing piece covered with the same icing; a party with the kids at an nearby orphanage in which only anchovy pizza was served; and a pair of aluminum crutches to play around the house during her free time. Her parents were very pragmatic and didn't argue with her. The cake arrived with a missing piece, ten large anchovy pizzas were delivered, and two aluminum crutches with a red ribbon turned up by her bedroom door early morning.

The reason that compelled Nastaran to study parapsychology in college is unclear. One could assume that the young woman was very curious or innovative, and that her parents' distaste for complications had made it easier for her to pick a career so fascinating, but at the same time so uncertain. Uncertain? Nastaran didn't like that term. She felt it was inaccurate, pretentious, and unfair. Scholars argue that the use of experimental methodologies instead of the accepted scientific method hinders the acceptance of parapsychology as a science. Scientists demand that disciplines generate some demonstrable theory through the scientific method to be considered as sciences. Since parapsychologists have failed in their attempts to present such a theory, the impassive scholars continue to call it a pseudoscientific discipline.

Nastaran always resented that judgement. She felt a disfavor of that kind required concrete actions at the level of those who conceived it, and from the beginning of her studies in the distant Scotland, she

Roberto Porta-Córdoba

sought to find answers in the meanderings of uncertainty. She was always an exceptional student and in her senior year she had the opportunity she longed for, the opportunity not only to vindicate parapsychology, but also to expose herself to the paranormal events that had eluded her since childhood. Nastaran traveled back to the United States representing her college, and between conferences and seminars was interviewed by the Edward Rudi Educational Foundation. This organization was dedicated to educate and alert the public about the risks of accepting fiction as reality and investigated the study of paranormal phenomena under scientifically controlled conditions. Since its inception, the foundation had offered a million dollars to anyone who could prove a paranormal phenomenon under their strict settings, and up until now no one had been able to claim the offer.

Nastaran got down to business. She didn't waste a single minute. The brilliant student immediately thought of the famous Vriendschap house incidents, an alleged supernatural case in Long Island, thirty miles outside of New York City, and which she had proposed to investigate as part of her graduation thesis. She had chosen the case, not only for its paranormal allure, but also out of convenience. Her childhood home was only 50 miles west, in New Jersey, and she could comfortably and inexpensively work on her findings from there. Nastaran made sure that the case complied with the requirements imposed

123

by the skeptical foundation: a verifiable place with a history of paranormal activity that could be recorded, measured, and documented. When she consulted with her thesis advisors back in Scotland, they concluded she had nothing to lose. Her graduation thesis would be greatly enriched by the application of the investigative methods, instruments, and observations projected. Moreover, there was a possibility of collecting tangible evidence for the famed foundation, which could catapult parapsychology to levels never heard, in addition to bumping Nastaran' bank account without a guilty feeling, and maybe, just maybe... experience fear for the first time in her life.

The property in question was a Dutch Colonial-style house built in the twenties on a waterfront estate in a small town of Long Island, which was said to be haunted since 1974. The house was the scene of a mass murder, in which a young man shot dead his parents and his siblings while they slept because "voices in the home convinced him to do it." The house, with its 3 floors, 5 bedrooms, 3.5 bathrooms, a basement, a swimming pool, a boathouse, and a gambrel roof, remained empty after the gruesome killings for a whole year. It wasn't until the perpetrator was sentenced and put in jail that the house was sold to a couple with three children. Although the couple was informed about the murders, the bargain was too good to pass up, but the family ended up fleeing the house in terror 28 days later.

Roberto Porta-Córdoba

The family reported paranormal activity that included a garage door opening and closing by itself; slamming doors at night; cold spots in specific areas of the house; slime oozing out of keyholes; strange odors; the father waking up at 3:15 every morning, the precise time of the murders; his wife levitating off their bed; swarms of houseflies in the rooms despite being winter; and a priest who came to bless the house feeling a slap on his face while a male voice told him to get out.

The house remained vacant for another year, while hordes of thrill seekers dropped by just to peek at what quickly became "America's most haunted house". Eventually, a couple ventured to purchase the property at a low price, but the dozens of articles written about the house and the televised reports about the case had an irreversible effect. A book about the paranormal activities in the house was published and a movie was released shortly after, causing people to flock to the Vriendschap neighborhood just to gawk at the property. The house had also become infamous on an international level; dark tourists would stop to take pictures, people would stop to yell obscenities at it, even tearing pieces of the house as souvenirs, and drunken locals would gather outside the property at night shouting for the several characters of the movie to come out. It was too much for the new buyers, who despite police presence had to leave the house after nine sleepless nights while surrendering the bargain back to the bank.

Nastaran and her thesis companions traveled to the U.S. in the spring of 1982. The plan was to spend two nights at the haunted house and then a week at her home in New Jersey to assort all the data collected and work with the team. Her parents were ecstatic to have her around for a few days and had already prepared the place to accommodate Nastaran and her team. After a couple of days of recreation and legal paperwork, the students got to see the infamous house in Vriendschap. An ominous feeling seized them as soon as they got off the cab. The house looked in good shape and identical to the pictures they had seen, but it certainly had an unnerving aura that turned their excitement to apprehension by the time they finished taking pictures and exploring the exterior.

Those who accepted to accompany Nastaran in this endeavor knew that they would be subjected to an excruciating task, an exhaustive observation, and a research of unpredictable outcome. Nastaran was tough and thorough. From the beginning of her studies, she had unveiled fraudsters and discredited dozens of statements, cases, and manifestations presented as paranormal events at different venues in Europe. He had an excellent reputation in her young career, which extended well beyond the university circles of Scotland. As wishful as she was to encounter the unknown and face the otherworldly, she always privileged facts and evidence, even if her findings deflated her illusions time and again.

Roberto Porta-Córdoba

The research team was made up of Nastaran, a Scottish male student, a Hungarian male student, an Afghan female student, a Canadian female student, and a childhood friend from New Jersey whose only knowledge of parapsychology came from a course on mental control he had taken, which was very popular at the time. Why was this friend part of the team? Because –just like her parents- Nastaran was very practical. The friend had lived in the area all his life, knew the house's background very well, and was the owner of a van, the only vehicle large enough to accommodate six people, the cameras, tripods, microphones, sensors, lamps, infrared lenses, batteries, and cumbersome equipment needed for the observation… at no cost.

The crew left New Jersey in the direction of Long Island one early afternoon. Although the house still had beds and chairs, the bank's permit did not allow the use of any furniture or appliance and had restricted the visit to just one night. A security guard from the bank would keep watch outside. The team carried sleeping backs, blankets, and a cooler with food and beverages. They had arranged a schedule so each crew member could sleep two hours. Nastaran reminded her colleagues that the last family who inhabited the house had not reported any supernatural events, and that the last report of paranormal activities had been filed by the previous owners. The team was eager and ready.

Leaving early proved wise. On the highway to Long Island, traffic slowed down almost to a halt. Apparently, there was an accident ahead, although no police lights were visible. The van kept moving slowly and after a few minutes they reached the point of the accident. A yellow cab had crashed into the back of a pickup truck and a pregnant woman laid on the bed of the pickup truck screaming at the top of her lungs. It was an emergency delivery and several people were trying to help her. Although the accident wasn't fatal, it made the woman panic and sent her into labor prematurely among all the confusion and commotion. The scene was surreal. The woman's screams pierced the air in a mix of fear and pain. Fortunately, as traffic kept moving, Nastaran saw ambulance lights approaching from the back and felt relief knowing the woman would get help. However, the woman's precarious situation and the screams were disturbing to her. They sounded like a mournful wailing that still resonated in her head after several miles, and gave her an odd sense of melancholy.

When the van got off the highway, in the direction of the Vriendschap area, the crew took notice of several homeless people on a sidewalk, lying down on cardboard next to a chain link fence. The red light allowed them to closely observe them from their seats. There were two older men smoking and laughing while drinking off plastic cups; a man with a thick bushy beard in squatting position listening to a portable radio and looking at a newspaper; a skinny woman

128

comforting a man wearing a basketball jersey, who rubbed the back of his head looking down at the sidewalk, and a shirtless man in a baseball cap sitting against the fence, staring at the cars on the street. Despite the chilly weather of early spring, none of them seem to care. A few blankets, plastic jugs, and old bags were scattered around them. Nastaran and the others freaked out when the man in the baseball cap suddenly got up furiously and started cursing and kicking the two older men lying on the sidewalk. He looked completely spaced-out and could barely stand on his feet, but he continued to kick aimlessly in the direction of the others, while the skinny woman and one of the men got a hold of him. The man with the thick bushy beard noticed the passengers in the van watching the scene. He pointed at the vehicle with an angry face, stood up, and started to walk defiantly toward the van. At that moment, the light turned green and the vehicle was able to move on with their frightened passengers, but the man got so close to the window that Nastaran made contact with his menacing blue eyes. She felt a sensation of creepiness she hadn't felt in a long time.

By the time the team got to the house, the afternoon was dripping away. They hurried to set all the equipment around as planned. Nastaran knew the house blueprints very well and made sure the team got organized without much delay. Her companions look a little nervous after a few minutes inside the place. It was damp and smelly. All the fuss about the hauntings

129

had dwindled a bit and at least that evening there were no drunkards shouting in front of the house. However, some of the hate graffiti was still visible on the outside walls, and the pair of quarter-moon shaped windows in the attic that resembled a pair of spooky eyes were still there. It didn't help that the surroundings were quiet and dark.

The observation began at eight o'clock. Nastaran recorded an introduction, issued the final directions, and distributed the team in three pairs, one on each floor. The murders had been committed in the bedrooms of the second and third, and that's where Nastaran mounted the recording cameras. Only the minimum required lights were left on. Outside, the assigned security guard sat in his parked vehicle, at Nastaran's request.

Nothing happened during the first hour. The only audible noises came from the sporadic wind outside moving the tall trees and the lazy tires of the infrequent cars caressing the pavement as they drove by. The foreign students, still tense but more adapted, sat in semi-darkness looking silently at the windows and the hallway. While her childhood friend stood downstairs peeking out the window and caressing a bat he was carrying, Nastaran remembered the scene of the homeless people and the startling fight they had witnessed. How many poor souls lived in those conditions in Long Island? Wasn't there a place in the whole state of New York that could help these people? Wasn't the United States the richest nation in the

130

world? She clearly remembered the expression on the bearded man's face as he approached the van earlier. It was a look of hopelessness and resentment.

It was around nine when they heard a scream. A distant, faint yell, coming from the direction of the waterfront. It didn't sound alarmed. It rather sounded like drunken revelry or a person calling someone at distance. The team remained quiet. The scream reminded Nastaran of the pregnant woman on the highway yelling on the bed of the pickup truck. Although different, the screams sounded similarly harmless. Was she alright? Had she given birth without complications? How was the newborn? For the first time in a while, Nastaran wasn't totally focused while working.

The next two hours continued in silence, broken only by the whispers of the team members communicating what was absolutely needed, or by the gentle steps of Nastaran ambulating slowly around the house. No paranormal events, no spirits, no devils, no ghosts. Around midnight, the team changed the recording tapes with perfect timing. The students were hungry and quietly munched on some of the sandwiches and drinks they had brought in. Their apprehension had gone away by this time and a couple of them started to yawn. The only nuisance was the cold which had slowly seeped into the house.

Around 1:00 am, Nastaran' childhood friend called her downstairs. He was not a student and he was not used to these long, passive observations. He was

131

obviously bored. The friend proposed something and asked Nastaran to let him try it. He suggested a more inductive approach with the hopes of "rattling" things a bit. Nastaran was not entirely convinced, she spurned improvisations, but after consulting with the others, she felt they could trust his friend's good judgement. Five hours had passed and not a single paranormal hint of activity had occurred in the house. Nastaran accepted. An unusual bad call.

After everyone returned to their spots, the friend started to raise his arms slowly with his eyes closed, and after a few minutes in a trance-like posture, the man started speaking, first softly then loudly. He was invoking the spirits. He was inviting them to manifest themselves, promising "understanding, empathy, and support." The night silence shattered like a giant pane of glass. The students felt puzzled and even scared, especially when the man –still with his eyes closed- shouted to "any surrounding entity" to come over them immediately, since they "meant no harm" and were there to "help them". Nothing happened. Denied and disappointed, the friend got irritated and started to scorn the spirits, calling them "cowards and ungrateful". Risking a twisted ankle, Nastaran darted down the stairs from the third floor and politely asked her childhood friend to put an end to his intervention. She felt embarrassed. She felt mortified.

Another hour went by in total silence again, but around 2:00 am a distinctive thump came from one of

132

the rooms on the second floor. The Afghan student clapped a hand over her mouth to stifle a whimper. Her Scottish partner alerted the others. His voice sounded hoarse and cracked. Nastaran summoned her friend with the bat and asked him to follow her into the room. Everyone glanced at each other frantically. The Canadian student tried to stop Nastaran in the hallway, but she easily went around her and peeked into the room using a mirror tied to a broomstick. While her childhood friend waited outside ready to swing the bat, Nastaran walked inside. Everyone held their breath. After a few seconds that felt eternal, Nastaran walked out with a stern face. There was no paranormal activity. She explained in a low voice that a camera cover had fallen off the tripod, bringing down with it the blank VHS tape they would use next. Everyone went back to the assigned spots, not without a bit of edginess. Nastaran was disappointed.

As planned, the team met on the first floor at 3:00 am, while the cameras kept rolling. As mentioned, the father always woke up at 3:15 am feeling an eerie presence and hearing noises. Also, the three o'clock hour was popularly associated with supernatural events and was considered a witching time known as the "the devil's hour." Nastaran had long dismissed that story as mere folklore, but subconsciously held a slim hope that a paranormal activity would ensue. Nothing happened. When their watches signaled 3:20 am, they all resumed their spots. Nastaran began to grow disillusioned.

133

A little after 4:00 am, another scream was heard in the distance. Unlike the earlier one, this one sounded distressed, and it came from the opposite direction. It sent shivers down everyone's spine, except down Nastaran's and the Hungarian student who was already snoozing and didn't hear it. The scream was followed by a second one, a bit fainter. Drunkards? Revelers? Again? Everyone was attentive and tense, but after a few minutes of nervous breathing, the thick silence descended on the house again. For the next two hours nothing changed, other than the cold getting worse. One last time, the team needed to place blank tapes in the cameras. Oddly, Nastaran continued to lose focus. Coffee had kept her well awake, but her legs and back hurt a little. Her mind drifted a bit to a recurrent dream she occasionally had, in which she attempted to walk fast in an open field but wasn't able to, feeling as if she was walking in mud. The nocturnal observation was filling her with a sense of futility, a sense of ineffectiveness, a sense of stagnation. She felt her inquisitiveness draining out, and that really troubled her.

Around 6:45 am, the sound of smooth rolling of rubber against asphalt returned. A car passed by while Nastaran peeked through a window on the third floor and gazed out at the dawning sky. When she heard ducks quacking in the air and the distant vroom of a motorcycle in some street nearby, she knew it was over. It was time to turn off the cameras, disconnect the equipment, and pack up. By this time, the Afghan student had long fallen into the land of dreams, just like the Canadian student on the second floor. Nothing had happened. No paranormal events, no spirits, no devils, no ghosts.

As previously arranged with the bank, Nastaran's childhood friend came out of the house at 7:00 am to call the security guard and walk the perimeter of the property as well as the interior of the house to verify everything was in order. The grass felt soggy beneath their feet and the humidity smelled of pungent manure. While the crew disassemble the cameras and equipment, the guard and Nastaran walked the three floors and took care of the paperwork. As everyone exited the house and the guard locked the door, they saw a couple of police cars slowly drive by on a near street. The security guard told Nastaran that something had happened in an apartment a couple of blocks away from the house.

While helping the team load the van, Nastaran was pensive. She had come to terms with the fact that no paranormal phenomena had occurred during the observation, but her investigative obstinacy still held on to a couple of possibilities: teleportation and time travel. She recalled a fiction story by Colombian Nobel Prize winner Gabriel García Márquez, in which a couple sleeps in the bedroom of an old castle and wakes up in a different room, where a bloody murder had been committed years before. She also recalled the famous Vidal Case, a connoted but fraudulent teleportation event in Argentina that she had analyzed

135

in a case study. Nastaran was convinced that some biblical passages contained examples of teleportation, as when Jesus rescued the frightened apostles on the boat buffeted by winds and the boat immediately appeared at the land to which they were going (John 6: 16-21). Could Nastaran and her crew have been teleported to another place, overnight? Would they realize that they were not really in the Vriendschap area as they drove away? Would they find themselves living in the past? Would the radio station in the van played old music or mention an old date?

To parapsychologists, predictable and ordinary things are as unsettling as they are for poets, except that poets don't carry the burden of proof when they write about their clouds "crying in sadness" or their oceans "boiling with each sunset." Unfortunately for Nastaran, no teleportation or time travel had taken place, either. She observed the very same trees and the same neighborhood she had seen the day before, and the radio broadcast mentioned the correct date. To make things worse, Nastaran's childhood friend began to fall asleep at the wheel after a few minutes and she had to take over the driving responsibility.

As she drove out of Long Island and before getting on the interstate, Nastaran stopped to buy some doughnuts and coffee for the homeless people they had seen the afternoon before. She wasn't hungry and everyone in the van was sleeping. When she passed by the same corner, she found it empty. There were still a couple of shabby blankets and a plastic bucket left on

Roberto Porta-Córdoba

the sidewalk, but none of the homeless fellows were there. Nastaran had no choice but to sip coffee all the way home.

One last task was pending: checking the eleven hours of videotaped material from the three cameras used. The job had been set up for the following day so that everyone could get some rest, but it was not in Nastaran's nature to leave passion for the unreliable tomorrow. After the team got back home, she sent everyone to their rooms and took a power nap, then she showered, got dressed, and quickly set up the equipment and screens to play the three tapes simultaneously. By the time the other students began to wake up late in the afternoon, she had already gone through five hours of videotape without detecting anything unusual. She hoped to notice something on the videos that could have escaped their attention the night before, some minor paranormal activity, a sign, an odd figure, a light, a noise... anything, but so far she had only heard the 9 pm faint scream in the distance, some whispering from members of the team, and her own voice giving directions at different times.

Despite everyone's pleas, Nastaran declined to go out with the team that night. She was not in the mood and preferred to continue watching the videos. The other students took a break and went out with her childhood friend, who served as a guide. Nastaran continued to watch the videos attentively and focused, moving her eyes from screen to screen rapidly and alertly, minute after minute, hour after hour, looking

137

for any sign of paranormality or spiritual manifestation. At times, she would stop the tapes to rewind them and watch a segment again, but all her efforts proved fruitless as nothing unusual turned up on the videos. She cringed when she watched the unfortunate intervention of her childhood friend appealing to the spirits and paid close attention when she heard the two distant screams recorded around 4:00 am. It was a little after midnight when the videos reached the end. Nastaran had not seen or heard anything she could consider supernatural or otherworldly. She had no substantial evidence of paranormal activity. Frustrated, she came to grips with not having anything at all.

Nastaran was exhausted. Her eyes burned, but she wasn't sleepy. For the first time in a while, she felt hungry. She moved to the kitchen, but didn't turn on the lights. A feeling of gloom descended on her. The house was quiet. Her parents wouldn't be home until the following day. In the semidarkness, she spotted a cake on the table. It was missing a piece, the one she had taken to the old house for a snack. She also noticed the newspaper, already out of its plastic wrap because her inevitable childhood friend had removed the sports page. She picked it up while opening the refrigerator to grab a slice of old anchovy pizza from two nights before and turned on the TV in the living room. Her parents were cable subscribers and Nastaran flipped pass a new channel called MTV which broadcasted music videos 24 hours a day. She couldn't understand

Roberto Porta-Córdoba

who would want to watch music videos round the clock and moved on to the local news channel.

She was reheating the slice of pizza in the kitchen when she heard something in the broadcast that got her attention. She poked her head in the living room and watched in disbelief the news of a 78 year old man whose dead body had been found by his daughter. Police officials said the man had died of natural causes over a year before and his corpse was in advanced state of decomposition. The daughter had driven from her home in Delaware after she was contacted by welfare services about the unpaid portion of the apartment's rent. She and her brother had a strained relationship with their father and had not seen him in a couple of years. The daughter thought her brother was taking care of the rent portion assigned to his father and the brother thought that his sister was doing it. The electricity and water had not been cut off because they were automatically debited off the man's retirement account. When the daughter made it to the apartment around 4:00 am, she let out a scream of horror after forcing her entry and finding his father' decaying body sitting on the couch next to a newspaper from a year before. The news broadcast described how the woman, repelled by the sight and the stench of death, had run back outside yelling in hysteria before the startled neighbors called police. Nastaran gasped when the news report revealed the apartment address to be two blocks away from the house where she and her team had spent the night conducting the

139

observation. The two screams heard and recorded around that time had come from the woman.

Nastaran felt an unfamiliar sensation of dread run through her body as she nervously stood in front of the TV. Before she could assimilate what she had just watched, the following news event unsettled her completely. It showed a group of homeless people being removed by the city from a sidewalk in Long Island after one of them suffered a fatal accident. Nastaran immediately recognized the corner where they had seen the homeless the day before. What the broadcast showed next left her stunned. The face of the bushy-bearded man she had seen up close while in the van appeared on the TV screen. It was from an expired driver's license. The news anchor reported that the man had angrily run onto the street chasing another homeless who had taken a newspaper from him, and had been mangled by the wheels of a passing garbage truck. Below the picture were the name and age of the unfortunate man, but all what Nastaran could focus on were his penetrating blue eyes.

Shaken up, she turned off the TV and sat on the sofa. She was speechless. She was astonished. However, a moment later, she got up. Her methodical temperament wouldn't allow emotions to get in her way. She grabbed the newspaper again and walked back to the kitchen, but she couldn't eat the slice of pizza. Her appetite was gone. With the images of the newscast still flashing in her head, she opened the newspaper and nervously browsed through several

140

pages, as if trying to reset her mind, as if trying to erase what she had just seen. She kept browsing aimlessly, until one of the headlines caught her eye. She froze. Right there, on the local news page, was a picture of the accident from the afternoon before between the cab carrying the pregnant woman and the pickup truck, the accident they had come across on the highway. Nastaran panted in disbelief as she read how the woman had been taken off to three different hospitals after the first two rejected her for not having medical insurance, and how the woman had died from complications caused by the delay in delivering a healthy baby.

Nastaran started to sob uncontrollably. A sensation of calamity and spookiness embraced her. For the first time in her life she felt fear. The fear that no ghostly presence had ever instilled in her. The fear that her unquenchable pursuit of the supernatural had never granted her. Soon, her sobbing turned into weeping, and the weeping into a loud scream, and into another, and into another. She felt a nauseating mixture of sorrow, helplessness, and anger.

After a while, Nastaran calmed down. She sat on a kitchen stool. She breathed in deeply, her heart beating fast, the big lonely house as her only companion. Her parent's house. Her childhood home. She laid eyes on the cake with the missing piece on the table, and then on the uneaten slice of anchovy pizza on a plate. She remembered when she was little. Slowly, but knowing what she wanted, she walked up

141

the stairs and through the dark hallway to her bedroom, the same one she had occupied since infancy. She opened her old closet and searched.

When the other students and the childhood friend returned to the house minutes later, they observed in amazement the silhouette of a woman in crutches wandering the second floor corridor at high speed.

Nastaran always finished what she started, so she went on to complete her college degree and graduated as a parapsychologist with the highest academic honors at her university in Scotland. However, she never practiced the profession. She went back home to New Jersey and obtained a master's degree in social work and a doctorate in education. Eventually, she moved to Virginia and has been happily teaching and working with disadvantaged kids ever since. No ghost has crossed her path, yet.

Enter Amalia

No, bro. I really don't know what Amalia meant to me. Let alone what I meant to her. That's in the past. Water under the bridge. Why talk about it, then? One, because I ran into her last week. Two, because she's part of the story of my life. Three... because you asked me.

The only thing I know for sure is that –at least in those days- she meant something to me. I was lonely, restless, disoriented, insecure... I had a complex about my size... I had a complex about the color of my skin... I had a complex about my accent. Stupidities, you know. Dumb stuff. Maybe Amalia helped me fight off those negative feelings. I don't know.

I met her at the bank where I was working back then. In Orlando, bro. The O-Town, yeah. You already know that I came from Puerto Rico when I was young. I was 18. I had studied English in high school, but we never progressed beyond the verbs "to be and "to do". That was all what English teachers taught us every school year, every grade, every semester, you know. When I came here, I had to take English courses before attending college. I felt I didn't fit at the bank. I didn't have any problems at home, or in the neighborhood. My insecurity was only at work. Maybe because my coworkers were all white. Even the Hispanics, the other Puerto Ricans. They were white as sugar.

I was the only one with light brown skin. And I had an accent in English that could often turn really heavy. I mispronounced a lot. Sometimes, my buddies at work would make fun of me, but I didn't get pissed off. They didn't mean any harm. I just laughed it off, you know. Sometimes I mispronounced "sheet" as "shit", "beach" as "bitch", and "peace" as "piss". The guys at the bank cracked up laughing every time.

I remember a word that I used very often. I don't even remember where I got it from, but instead of simply saying that I was happy about something, I would say "I'm elated." Those jerks would die laughing and even begged me to repeat it. And not to mention when I mispronounced the branch manager's last name, Mr. Fox, as something naughty. Bro! They would go nuts laughing. Idiots. They really liked to tease me! But it was just for fun. Jokes, you know. Although, sometimes I think that so many jokes subconsciously developed a complex in me. I was the Puerto Rican newcomer. They were the English speaking sons and daughters of Hispanic immigrants, born and raised in the U.S.

My coworkers respected me, you know, but didn't invite me into their inner circle. They never asked me to join them when they went clubbing. They only invited me when they played baseball or basketball after work. Never on weekends. But I didn't really care, man. I had my own buddies to hang out with on the weekend, but, you know, deep down I didn't feel the same as the guys at the bank. We all wore the same starched white shirts and the same ties, but the female cashiers didn't pay much attention to me. They were polite, but never engaged in long conversations with me. I don't know, bro. I felt weird.

It was then when I ran into Amalia, a tall, slim brunette, with long curly hair and thick lips. She was

144

born in Venezuela, but her parents moved to Florida when she was two years old. The first time she came to the bank for training, she was wearing spandex pants with a little skirt on top and huge hoop earrings. I mean… huge, bro! But, that was the fashion in the late 80s, you know. The Jodi Watley look. I think that little skirt on top of the pants was what caught my attention.

Amalia was friendly and sweet. She looked sharp and attractive in the bank's cashier uniform. She was great with customers. Everyone liked her. Maybe that was why I felt lucky when they assigned her to assist me with document filing during slow times, you know, those hours when there are few or no customers in line. I felt as if the bank was integrating me to the cool, to the modern… to the fashionable. You see how stupid I was, man? Talk about insecurity, bro!

To my surprise, Amalia liked me. At the beginning, I thought that it was only because she was nice and kind to everyone, but another cashier who knew her told me that she'd said I was a nice guy. The same cashier told me that Amalia had recently broken off with her boyfriend and that maybe I should ask her out. Can you imagine, bro? I felt freaking lucky! And let me tell you something, man. I could've been an insecure moron, but I was not slow! When I saw the opportunity to go out with the hottest chic at work, you bet I took it! The following week I asked her out and… you know what she said to me? She said: "Oh, Manolo, why hadn't you asked me out before?" I couldn't believe it, man. I get goosebumps just remembering! You know what that meant to me at that time…? You don't know squat, bro. Here I am telling you a story and you're playing Fortnite, like a teenager! You really suck, dude!

That's how I started to date Amalia. In some occasions, she would wear the spandex pants with the little skirt. People stared at her at the mall, in the restaurants, and everywhere we went. It probably had to do with her resemblance to Jody Watley or simply because she had a great body. And I liked that, bro! It made me feel proud, you know. I enjoyed the attention she got.

Sex? I knew you would ask, pervert. But, I'm not going to talk about it. You know why? For three reasons: first, because sex has nothing to do with this story... second, because only scumbags and lowlife cowards share with others what they do with their girl... and third, because I don't freaking feel like it, damn it!

Amalia was cool, bro. She was pretty and smart. She was going to college! She wanted to be a teacher, you know. She loved kids. To me, that was perfect. People liked her as soon as they saw her. My girlfriend was popular, you know. But, now that I look back, I realize how big of moron I was. I went out with her because I liked her, but also because I wanted people to see me with her. You know what I mean, bro? Was I dumb or what?

I felt that Amalia made up for my shyness and my insecurities... When I was with her, I felt more socially accepted, more connected... I felt cool. She taught me to eat things that I didn't eat before: arepas, sushi, Indian food... She was simple, but she had manners. She taught me to act with finesse at the dining table, to use the silverware in the proper

146

sequence… the cups… the napkins. It was like taking a course in etiquette, man!

She convinced me to go back to college. That's how much influence she had on me. I had dropped from college two years before and I always said I would go back, but never did, until Amalia practically dragged me into the registrar's office, spoke for me, got all the information I needed, and registered me. I started playing sports again and going to the gym with some of the guys from work. All of a sudden, I felt as if they had accepted me, or maybe it was just my imagination. Maybe they had never rejected me. Maybe I was the one who had self-excluded. I don't know, man. When I began to gain muscles, Amalia bought me tight t-shirts and pullovers. I looked good, bro. I felt good.

My music taste also changed. Before meeting Amalia, I only listened to that freestyle music of the 80s, the one we played with the boom-box, groups like Planet Patrol, Exposé, Fun Fun, TKA, or what people now call "one-hit wonders". Before meeting her, I wore gold chains, half-buttoned shirts with the sleeves rolled up, white shoes without socks, and I sprayed myself with Calvin Klein's Obsession cologne. Can you picture that, bro? When I started going out with Amalia, I learned to listen to salsa, merengue, rock, and even classical music. I started to dress with more variety and more formality.

Amalia changed my life, man, or maybe I didn't have one before. I mean a social life, balanced, healthy… normal. That's why, years later, when she was already gone and I had graduated from college, I thought about writing my autobiography in the future,

147

when I got old, you know. I decided that I would reserve a chapter for that period of my life and I would title it "Enter Amalia". Can you imagine? Already graduated, with an improved English, and thinking about writing a book! Of course, I never wrote a darn page, but somehow the title of the chapter stuck in my memory.

The only thing I never negotiated with her was the "Miami Vice" show. No way! I convinced her to watch it with me every Friday before going out. I'm not talking about the movie that came out after. I'm talking about the TV show that ran for five years until 1989. Dan Johnson, Phillip Michael Thomas, the music, the cars, the streets of Miami… oh, man! Those were the times, bro!

But, what can I say, man? At the end, I behaved like a jerk. I turned jealous, we started to argue for little things and before I knew it, we were fighting over everything. I knew it was over one night that she left me waiting for her at a rock concert. She had to run some errands first with her mom and we had agreed to meet at the stadium gates. Cellphones were not around yet. Only beepers, you know. I had stopped using mine because Amalia found them tacky. Drug dealers used them a lot back then and she didn't want me to look like one. I couldn't contact her. I watched the concert alone. Puzzled. Angry. Things got worst and by the end of the year we weren't an item anymore. We broke up.

At the beginning, I didn't miss Amalia that much. We kept a professional and respectful relationship at work. Since I already dressed and acted like the others, I had made more friends. I partied

148

every weekend and began dating other girls. But, it felt weird. We humans are strange, bro, I'm telling you. I began to get bored with all the partying, the drinking, and the long nights. I wanted to have a formal relationship again. Slowly, I realized that I missed Amalia. I asked her out one day, but she turned me down. She said that although I wasn't a bad person, I had been very rude to her, and that sometimes I acted with selfishness, arrogance, and disregard for other people. She said that many times I had been ordinary and tacky. What the hell? What did she mean by that, bro? Ordinary? Tacky? I remembered I took it really bad and spent the weekend pissed off. I felt rejected. Totally dissed.

She left the bank shortly after that. She said goodbye to me as if nothing had happened. Several coworkers invited for drinks after her last day at work. I didn't go. I don't remember why. I might have been busy or maybe my pride didn't let me.

Time passed by and I was promoted to branch assistant manager. I started to make more money, bro. A few months later I bought a townhouse in a nice Orlando area and continued dating and partying with moderation. But I felt I had lost something. People always asked me about Amalia and when I told them that we had broken up, the idiots always said "Ooooh… what a pity… she was such a nice girl… she was a sweetheart" and looked at me with regret.

Eventually, I took her out of my system, bro. Time heals everything, you know. Little by little my pride recovered, I got over all my stupidities, and I married the girl who is now my wife. As you can see, things have gone well for us. I'm the branch manager

149

now. I heard that Amalia also got married and was doing well. I suppose that my obsession with her was aggravated by my former low self-esteem. I now think that once I got over those insecurities, I stopped needing her.

Fate had it that I came across her one more time. It was at a wedding, last week. The wedding of a common friend who held the reception in a fancy place downtown. When we met at the lobby, I introduced her to my wife. Amalia introduced me to her husband. I was nervous at first, man. I didn't know how Amalia was going to react, but everything went nice and smooth. We sat at different tables.

Almost at the end of the meal, I felt the crown that replaced one of my back molars get loose. It had happened to me before and I dreaded having to go back to the dentist. I hate going to any doctor, bro! I hurried to the restroom to check my mouth and when I came out to the hall Amalia was standing outside the men's restroom, with her back turned and looking at her phone, waiting for her husband to come out. Her body had changed. She had lost some of her waist and her calves looked muscular. I noticed that her bearing was not the same. She didn't look tall. Her shoulders were droopy and her arms looked bony.

There was no one else in the hall. I had the opportunity to talk alone with her, but… about what, bro? What was I going to ask her? I swear, dude. At that moment, I no longer felt anything for Amalia. She was out of my system. It wasn't as if my heart was beating faster for an old flame or any of that nonsense. It was not. But a last minute impulse made me talk to her, say something to her. For an instant, I felt my
150

foolishness and insecurity coming back to me. I felt compelled to give her details about my life, tell her that I had a son, that my wife managed her owned beauty salon, that I had graduated from college and was being considered for a regional position at an important financial firm, that I drove a $90,000 car, that my house had a pool, and that I felt like a winner.

Amalia turned when I called her name. "Hi, Manolo!" she said with a kind smile. It was my chance, bro. My chance to put an end to a historic insecurity. My chance to demonstrate that I wasn't "ordinary" or "tacky"; my chance to subtly show her that I didn't need her anymore, that I had gotten over her, and that everything was fine.

I wanted to look and sound self-confident, relaxed, cool... as I really felt now. But, I couldn't, bro. Damn it! At the precise moment I was going to start talking, the stupid crown came off my molar and I felt it loose inside my mouth. I struggled to conceal it and tried to secure it with my tongue, but I couldn't. I almost swallowed it, man. I thought I was going to choke and couldn't avoid coughing. I tried covering my mouth with my fist, but it was too late. The fake tooth came out flying with a thread of saliva and blood, and landed on Amalia's foot. Can you imagine, bro?

She looked at me, startled, when I bent over to pick up the damn crown. I had blood on my lips. She looked at me in confusion at first, but then gave me that familiar icy look. I recognized it, bro. I remembered it. She softly stepped back with a condescending smile. At that precise moment, her husband came out of the restroom and greeted me with a pat on my arm. Smiling, he asked me something

151

about the reception, but I don't remember what it was, and I don't remember what I answered, either. I don't remember what I did or what happened after. I only remember that they disappeared down the hall and that I walked back into the bathroom like in a trance, feeling like an idiot, feeling like an imbecile.

Hoops and Solace

Every year we watched the NBA Finals together: the Fergusons, the Brooks, the Sandovals, and us. The Johnsons abandoned us when they moved out of state, but then we got the Baums and sometimes the Gallaghers. Most of the time, we saw the games at the Sandovals' home –Fernando prepared the best ribs in town-, but we also set camp at the Fergusons' a lot, especially after Glenn got that 27-inch flat-screen TV, a monster size at the time.

Victoria, my wife, didn't mind hosting our friends for the games, but we lived in a townhouse with a rather small living room, our TV set was not that big, and sometimes Jenna or little Thomas would wake up startled by the clapping and the loud gibberish caused by the game. That's why we never watched major sports events at home. We would ask my sister-in-law Clarissa to babysit and off we were to the Sandovals' house or wherever we had agreed to meet.

It was the 80s. The play-by-play announcer was always Dick Stockton and the analysts were either Bill Russell or Tom Heinsohn. For some reason Victoria disliked Heinsohn. Every time the poor fellow appeared on the screen she made derogatory remarks against the man. Maybe it had something to do with the fact that Heinsohn favored the Boston Celtics and Victoria rooted for any team that played against them. You see, back then, we didn't have a NBA team in Oklahoma City. We all supported teams from out of town.

153

Kevin's disappearance occurred during the 1987 Finals, by chance, the last Finals Heinsohn covered. It happened sometime during the third or fourth quarter of game 5, between the Los Angeles Lakers and the Celtics. I can't recall all the details now, but I remember most of us were in high spirits, anticipating a Lakers' win which would've ended the series.

I do remember we were at the Fergusons'. In addition to the big TV, the Fergusons' place was perfect to watch those games because it was the last house on the block, in a brand-new community still under construction, and with very few neighbors who could complain about our crazy and frequent uproars. Other than the poor street lighting which made the surrounding a bit dark, the place was great to barbecue, sip beer in the backyard, and scream to the top of our lungs, if needed.

According to the police report filed that night, Kevin had left the house through the sliding backdoor and walked to his car to retrieve a pack of cigarettes, but had never come back. His wife Goldie started to look for him after he failed to return for more than 20 minutes. I remember we teased her about Kevin taking a dump in the restroom and cruelly dismissed her worries with our eyes glued to the screen. However, as the game approached its final minutes without our friend coming back inside, one of us walked out the front door to look for him, playfully calling out his name and asking him not to be a party pooper right at that crucial moment of the game.

Grumbling about the Lakers not securing the title after losing to Boston, we gulped our last drinks

154

and remembered until then that Kevin's car was not parked in front of the Fergusons' house. He had parked by the empty lots next to it, where more single homes were being built, but his car was not there. At first, we thought he had probably run out of cigarettes and had driven to a convenience store.

"He's really addicted to those smokes," claimed Norman.

"I can't believe he couldn't wait until the game was finished," added Norman's wife.

I found it a little odd, but knowing how impulsive Kevin was at times, I kept telling his wife to relax. There were no cell phones back then, at least not available to regular folks like us, and Kevin didn't carry a beeper, which many of us used back then. We sat down and wrap up the last comments about the game, waiting for our friend to come back.

"He's a jerk!" began to complain Goldie. "How can he just drive for cigarettes or beer without letting me know?"

We just laughed it off and made fun about Kevin's "independence", how inspiring his example was to the rest of us married men, and other bad jokes. However, when a whole hour passed by without him coming back, I decided to go look for him at the nearby shopping plaza. Maybe he'd got a flat tire. Dennis and Norman drove with me, while asking our wives and the others to stay with Goldie.

"We'll bring you that moron right away," joked Dennis.

"I bet you he got pulled over by a cop and he's arguing with him about basketball," added Norman with a chuckle.

155

Fictions of an Immigrant

I know it's been over 30 years now, but I still remember the eerie feeling that seized me when we drove by the empty spot where Kevin had parked his car. I knew right then that something bad had happened to our friend. I still can't explain how I knew it. When we got to the convenience store, no one could give us a clue about Kevin. We started to get really concerned. We drove back slowly, paying attention to each car that came in the opposite direction. Kevin drove a distinctive car. It was a red Toyota Tercel disguised as a pacing car, with a lot of sporty stickers, large yellow numbers, and stuff. It was tacky and impossible to miss.

When we got back to the Fergusons', Goldie was hysterical. Her eyes were red from crying. The others had already called the police and the car description had been radioed to all patrols in the area. Obviously, something had happened to Kevin on his way to wherever he was going. The police declared him a "missing person" after 24 hours. We feared the worst when the car turned up semi-dismantled on interstate 44 two days later. The official version was that Kevin had been robbed and his car stolen, all in the context of a probable homicide.

The third day, the police located a couple of suspects through the fingerprints they had collected from the car's bodywork. It wasn't really that difficult. They confessed they had stolen the car from the Fergusons' neighborhood. Even though the detectives interrogated them thoroughly, they swore they had not wrestled the vehicle from Kevin. They maintained all along that they never came across him, never struggled with him, never met him, never saw him. They had

156

only stolen the car from the curbside where it was parked. Nothing could be proved otherwise. Public opinion was hard on the thieves. Most people didn't believe them. There was an outrage in town. Yet, they could not be found to be murderers. Kevin's whereabouts remained a mystery.

Goldie moved to Missouri after exhausting all means and hopes of finding out what had happened to her husband. She was never the same. None of us were ever the same, actually. We stopped watching the NBA Finals together. It brought sad and confusing memories. Eventually, we lost track of Goldie. The Sandovals moved to Nevada, the Brooks left for Oregon, and we didn't see much of the others, either. Until last week.

I received a phone call at noon. It was Victoria. She had been contacted by the Fergusons, whom we hadn't seen in months. They told her that Kevin's remains had been found, almost 32 years later.

It took us a while to fully comprehend what had happened. The fateful night of his disappearance, Kevin had fallen into a construction ditch near the house while taking a shortcut to his car. The position of his skeleton and a fracture on the skull showed that he hit one of the sides on the way down, causing the wall to partially collapse and bury him. The investigation later found out that when the workers resumed their work the following morning, they poured concrete for foundation columns into the ditch, as planned. Recent rebuilding work done at the property had revealed the gruesome sight of his remains along with a bottle of beer, a clasp-knife he always carried in his pocket... and his car keys. The

157

Fictions of an Immigrant

thieves didn't lie. They had stolen the car before Kevin got to it.

There will be a memorial service at the end of the week. The service our buddy never had. Goldie will attend. Part of the old gang will attend. I'm sure we will all feel a little better. Bringing closure to a tragedy like is certain to bring some solace to his family and to all of us. But just some solace. Just some.

For his family, Kevin will remain gone. A proper burial of his ashes, although dignifying, will not bring him back. For us, thinking about the despicable coincidence that his car was stolen around the same time he fell into that ditch is a calamity that makes it the most painful. Why did the thieves have to choose his car? Why did Kevin have to take a shortcut in the near dark? What if he was only unconscious after he fell into that hole and died later under the pile of earth because of his injuries? If his car had been there when the police arrived, the detectives would not have assumed that he drove off and most likely they would have focused the search in the immediate surroundings, way before the workers filled the ditch with the concrete. Inadvertently, the car theft might have served as a fatal and heartbreaking diversion of police resources and procedures. Sometimes, some solace is not solace. Not solace at all.

Roberto Porta-Córdoba

The Fine Art of Indiscretion

Ever since childhood in his native Honduras, Pedro had always been reckless. Without any malicious intent, but reckless. He had been indiscreet and sometimes a complete screw up. At the age of eight he got a spanking from his mother when a skinny lady dressed in black came to their house to present her condolences for the death of Pedro's grandmother, and Pedro, impressed by a tall fang that the woman had in her teeth, warned to her mother that someone was waiting for her in the living room, and when her mother asked who it was, he without any hint of malevolence had answered at the top of his lungs: "I don't know, but it's a lady who looks like a vampire."

In adulthood, Pedro improved his flaw a little. His marriage to Carolina had certainly settled him. Carolina was a reserved and unpretentious woman. She did not like Pedro telling spicy jokes, or using unnecessary adjectives to describe a situation or a person. Although outgoing and sociable, Carolina was very discreet and gently pinched her husband whenever she thought he was joking or talking too much.

-What happened? Why are you pinching me? – Pedro would ask.

-Because you said "paunchy" and the chubby man on the right glanced at you -Carolina would whisper in his ear.

159

Despite the progress, the couple was not entirely safe from Pedro's indiscretions. On one occasion, a Cuban coworker invited them to his home to meet his family. Pedro and Carolina were enjoying the food, drinks and attention. Carolina and the Cuban's wife were talking about their families and the conversation was going smoothly. The children and grandchildren of the hosts were also present and the Caribbean music in the background enlivened the environment. Then, the topic of the talk turned to the curious names that some people give their children.

-In Cuba, I met a boy named Usnavy González -said the host.

-And how did he get that name? -asked Pedro, laughing.

-In Batista's time, his father would see the ships of the American navy pass off the coast of Havana and he liked the large letters that said US NAVY with the colors of the flag –answered the Cuban host.

The worst case I heard was that of a Cuban in Miami who named his son Ledif, -Pedro replied-. He hated Fidel Castro so much that he spelled his name backwards: L-E-D-I-F. Can you imagine the poor boy with that horrible name?

Immediately, the eldest daughter of the host opened her eyes wide and turned to her father.

-You see, dad? You see? My name is awful!- she yelled, before storming out of the living room.

Carolina felt a stabbing, knife-like pain in her stomach. She wished she could turn into a mosquito

160

and fly away. Pedro wished he could turn into a cockroach and be squashed. There was a dreadful silence. It was horrible, just horrible.

But even with all their awkwardness, Pedro's gaffes had never caused resentment to anyone, nor loss of friendships, nor ruined opportunities for the couple. However, Carolina was persistent in demanding more caution from her husband. Over time, Pedro learned to joke or comment on things with more restraint and discretion. For a while, the embarrassing blunders seemed a thing of the past, until that bingo night at the school where Carolina worked.

On that occasion, they shared a table with another couple and their kids. They picked an area away from the stage to avoid the deafening sound of the huge loudspeakers at front. One of the topics of conversation at the table was the concert of Beyoncé, the famous R&B and hip hop singer scheduled for the following week. It was the first time the star was coming to Honduras and Pedro lamented that the tickets had sold out so fast. While Carolina, her friend, and the children were concentrating on the bingo, Pedro noticed that one of the event's presenters was Jefferson Medina, an acquaintance of his, and a well-known marketing manager for a successful transnational company.

- Is that Jefferson Medina? -Pedro asked his friend-. What is he doing up there?

-Yes, that's him -said the friend-. He's a member of the school's Parent Teacher Association.

161

You should go and ask him where to get tickets. His company is one of the concert sponsors.

Pedro thought it was a good idea, but he feared that if he asked him directly, Medina might think he was asking them for free. Many people did this with acquaintances in high positions and to Pedro it seemed a tasteless and abusive practice.

The bingo continued and the conversation took another turn, but it was then that Pedro noticed a young woman sitting next to an elegant older lady and a child at one of the tables in the front. "It's Maryann," he thought. "Medina's wife." The occasion came to mind when he and Carolina met Maryann and Medina at the movies and had decided to sit in adjacent seats. He remembered the pleasant chat the four of them had while waiting for the lights to go out. After that, he had only seen her at a Jefferson's birthday party several years before. Maryann looked the same to him, with the same straight light hair and the same slender figure she had at that time.

Pedro sat at the table and tried to pay attention to the bingo, but he was still thinking about the Beyoncé concert. He and Jefferson Medina had known each other since college and their work-related encounters had always been pleasant. Why not try to get those tickets? Carolina loved Beyoncé's music and had many of her songs in her playlist. Taking her to the concert would be a nice surprise.

-I'll be right back -said Pedro, getting up.

-Where are you going? -Carolina asked.

162

-I am going to walk around the tables and greet some friends – he replied.

-Sit down, honey. Enjoy the bingo, relax! –said Carolina, smiling -. You can do that later.

Pedro obliged and sat back down. He grabbed his cards back and resumed his play.

-I got three corners, look! –Carolina said with excitement-. One more and I win with this card!

-I don't have any luck with these things – complained her friend at the table-. I don't remember the last time I won at a bingo. Frank has better luck than me –she said, smiling at her husband.

-Not really –said the man, while several people yelled out bingo at another table-. See? That family has won like three times already.

Pedro smiled and got ready for the next game, but he wasn't really focused. The background music, the yelling, the bustle were louder and louder. They kept playing and were close to yell out bingo several times, with no luck. After a while, Pedro gave up. The Beyoncé concert kept coming back to him and decided he would try for those tickets. He got up from the table again.

-No luck tonight, folks –he said-. I'll be right back.

-Where are you going? –Carolina asked.

-I'd like to say hi to some people and greet the Medinas.

Carolina looked puzzled.

-Jefferson and Maryann, don't you remember them? –Pedro added.

-Not really -Carolina said, while turning to look in the direction that Pedro was pointing.

-Maryann is sitting at front. Let me say hi to her and then to Jefferson. I'll be right back –said Pedro.

-All right –Carolina said, while focusing on the bingo again-. Say hi to them.

Pedro walked to the front and greeted other acquaintances and parents from the school. He loved to socialize and enjoyed talking with people. As he approached the front of the auditorium, the volume of the loudspeakers and the intermittent music increased.

-Good evening! -he said to the young woman when he reached the front table, while greeting the elegant older lady and the child with a smile.

-Good evening -they answered, almost at the same time.

-How nice to see you again, Maryann! –Pedro said loudly, trying to talk over the loudspeakers and leaning down to kiss her cheek.

Then, he looked at the elegant older lady and gave her a big smile.

-I'm a friend of Jefferson and of your granddaughter –he said almost yelling.

He then greeted the child with a light pat on the head and smiled.

-Is this your girl, Maryann? She looks just like you –he said-. You are like two drops of water!

Roberto Porta-Córdoba

The young woman said something, but Pedro didn't hear her. The bingo numbers and noise from the speakers were too loud. He sat down on a chair next to her.

-Your girl is identical to you – he repeated-. She doesn't resemble Jefferson at all! And look at you! You look the same! You haven't changed a bit! –he said with a laugh.

Again, the young woman tried to say something, but Pedro was on a roll.

-We met your granddaughter and Jefferson at the movies –he said to the older lady-. They're a great couple!

The young woman leaned towards Pedro and talked in his ear. Pedro leaned his head to the side to hear her better.

-I'm not Maryann- she said-. Jefferson divorced her. I'm his girlfriend.

Pedro was silent for a second. He directed his gaze to the older lady and then to the girl.

-She's not my grandmother -the young woman added-. She's my mom. And he's not a girl. He's Jefferson's son.

Pedro felt a rush of heat on his face. He couldn't muster words. The older lady stared at him with a look of contempt. The boy, with his long fluffy hair, looked at him with disdain before shifting his attention back to his bingo cards. The young woman did not seem disgruntled, but she definitely seemed inconvenienced.

165

As if in a church, Pedro got up slowly from the table. He could've left it at that. Game over. End of the line. He could've simply said goodbye and walked away. He only needed to wring out a fake smile and leave. But, he didn't. Some people don't only invoke indiscretion. Some people make a fine art of it. Instead, Pedro leaned towards the young lady and put the cherry on the cake.

-I'm sorry... but it's just that... you look a lot like his ex-wife. I guess he has a very consistent taste – he said with sheepish eyes.

On the way back to his table, Pedro walked like in a daze. All the noises were gone. He felt as if moving in a tunnel of silence. He didn't want to make eye contact with anyone. He didn't want to talk to anyone. When he made it back, he sat with his back to the stage.

-Did you talk to Medina about the tickets? -his friend asked him in a low voice.

There are many tones of voice. Some can reveal a cold, others can reveal a feeling, others can reveal a mishap, and others can reveal... something. But when Pedro finally answered, his tone of voice didn't reveal anything. He sounded as if he were speaking in a different tongue.

-No, I didn't- he said-. I thought it would be an indiscretion.

Roberto Porta-Córdoba

Here Comes the Neighborhood

It was the championship game of the state of Indiana girls' volleyball tournament, and the arena was slowly filling up with fans from both finalist teams: Destiny High School from Indianapolis and Wabash River High School from Lafayette. For big games like this one, the league rented larger venues to accommodate the higher number of fans. Parents, siblings, and relatives of the players joined classmates, friends, and school staff members in an atmosphere of celebration and pride.

Pham Trong Linh was a Vietnamese man whose daughter Truc played the libero position for the Destiny HS team. Mr. Linh had dropped off his wife and children at the arena an hour earlier, and was back now looking for a parking space. After he found one, he noticed a black young man standing alone next to a luxurious Mercedes-Benz SUV parked beside. It seemed odd to him because the young man wasn't moving. He was just looking away attentively, as if waiting for something. Mr. Linh hesitated for a couple of minutes, but finally decided to lock his car and walk to the arena. As he passed some security guards at the entrance, he felt like telling them about the young man by the SUV, but finally decided not to. When he located his wife inside the arena, he told her he was worried because he'd seen a black teenager standing next to a high-end SUV parked next to their car. The wife frowned in concern and asked Mr. Linh what they should do about. He said he wasn't sure. "Check the car later to make sure everything is okay," the wife advised Mr. Linh.

The black young man was Olamide Brogdon, who had come with his family to support his cousin Aniyah, who played middle blocker for the Destiny HS team. He had been waiting inside his mom's SUV for Mrs. Galanis, the receptionist at his mom's dental clinic, whom Olamide's mom had invited to watch the game. Mrs. Galanis and her husband had just texted Olamide that they were driving into the parking lot, and Olamide had come out of the SUV to meet them and hand them their tickets. When they finally showed up. Olamide locked the SUV and walked with them to the arena. In the lobby, Olamide noticed that Destiny High School had placed a long table with pennants that had the school's logo on them. A sign said "one per fan." As Olamide grabbed one, a man in a baseball cap and a child approached the table and grabbed five pennants. The man spoke in Spanish to the kid and both walked away. Olamide shook his head in disbelief. When Olamide joined his family in the seats, he told them that a Hispanic man had taken five pennants in one shot, although he only had a child with him. One of Olamide's aunts grimaced in disapproval. "That man is an opportunist!" she said, "it's a different world these days, dear."

Ten rows above from where Olamide and his family were sitting, the Hispanic man was handing out the pennants to his companions. His name was

168

Roberto Porta-Córdoba

Anselmo Martinez and he was sitting with his wife, his elderly parents, his brother, his sister-in-law, and three children. A total of nine people. He distributed the banners only to the three kids and the elderly couple. They were proud and excited to see Anselmo's daughter, Violeta, play for the Destiny HS team. When Anselmo's wife asked him why he'd only brought five pennants, he answered, "Because I didn't want anybody to think I was an opportunist." Suddenly, a couple of bearded Arab men wearing white robes and skull caps sat next to them. The two men left an empty seat between them and briefly glanced at each other. Both of them had a backpack on their lap. Anselmo and his brother also glanced at each other. The backpacks had symbols all over and they looked bizarre to them. Anselmo elbowed his wife softly and whispered, "Uh, oh... I hope this arena had metal detectors at the gates."

The two men in thobes and kufis were from Qatar. They were professors at a university in their country and were attending a 3-week program at a university in Indiana that had a campus in Qatar. Their wives had stopped by the restroom with Rasha, the cousin of one of them. Rasha lived in Indiana and had invited the visitors to cheer for her niece, also a member of the Destiny HS team. When the two women joined their husbands in the seats, they claimed their backpacks from them. The backpacks, which they had bought in previous trip to Jordan, were beautifully embroidered in leather. The women wore their

169

traditional abayas and hijabs. Meanwhile, three white men and a woman sat in the row below them. Two of the men were covered in tattoos, one had a blond Verdi beard, and the woman had matching ear and nose piercings. The Qataris felt uncomfortable when the woman turned, looked at the backpacks and whispered something to the man next to her. Their discomfort turned to distress when the man also turned, smiled at them, looked at the backpacks and said something to the others. One of the Qatari said to his wife, "I think these ignorant jesters have never seen thobes before. They must be high on drugs, I can't believe they let them in like that. We'd better ignore them."

The two tattooed men and the woman were teachers at Destiny High School who had come to support their students. One of the men was an art teacher and piano player in his spare time, the other one was a counselor who also served as the director of student services, and the woman was a chemistry teacher, who also served as the science department chair and the school yearbook's advisor. The man with the Verdi beard was her boyfriend, who owned a small tech company and volunteered at local animal shelters on weekends. The woman had noticed the backpacks the Qatari women were carrying and had told her boyfriend how gorgeous they were. The art teacher, who had a master's degree in Arab studies and had traveled extensively in the Middle East, took a look at the backpacks and identified them as made in Jordan. He said they were handmade and a fine example of

Roberto Porta-Córdoba

Islamic art and craft. He promised to ask one of his Arab students' parents where they could get them. Minutes later, the Vietnamese man who had told his wife about the black teenager in the luxurious SUV, excused himself and his family as they squeezed pass the teachers on their way to their seats. "He stepped on my toe," the chemistry teacher said, chuckling. "Don't even think about complaining," her boyfriend joked. "He might set you straight with a karate move."

After a while, the arena lights dimmed and the championship game began. Fans of the Destiny HS team were mostly sitting on one side of the arena while fans of Wabash River HS were sitting on the other side. Both crowds were noisily cheering for their teams since the start of the match. Unfortunately for Destiny HS fans, their team was not playing well and lost two of the first three sets. Things turned grim when the Wabash River HS team took a 20-17 lead in the fourth set. It seemed that Destiny HS would have to settle with second place. The fans were still proud of their volleyball team and knew that this was just sports, but the Destiny HS side of the arena began to go quieter with disappointment and resignation.

All of sudden, when the scored reached 22-17 and only three points separated Wabash River HS from the state championship, one the tattooed teachers from Destiny High School got up in the stands and began to chant the teams' name. He started to wave his arms frantically asking everyone to stand up and cheer up the Destiny HS girls. At first, a few parents and fans followed, but when the girls scored three consecutive points and made the score 22-20, more people stood up and began yelling and cheering in support. A tall girl in the team, with the last name Brogdon on her jersey, who happened to be the black young man's cousin, got another point with a monster spike. The tattooed teacher started chanting her last name and in a few seconds most of the Destiny HS fans joined him in yelling "Brogdon! Brogdon! Brogdon!" Next, the Vietnamese man's daughter, made a fantastic block, and the Hispanic fans began chanting the name on her jersey: "Truc! Truc! Truc!" When the girls tied the game 22-22, the whole Destiny HS crowd was on their feet chanting the players' names off their jersey: "Martinez! Kowalski! Al-Madeed! Yang!

Eventually, the Destiny HS team tied the match 2-2 with a gutsy 25-23 come-from-behind win and prepared for the fifth and decisive set. Fans in the Destiny HS stands went wild. In a matter of minutes, the somber mood had turned into a frenzy and excitement ran high. The Arab men from Qatar high-fived the tattooed teachers on the row below and then knocked fist with the entire Martinez family next to them. Their wives clapped and nodded while a proud Anselmo kept telling them "That's my daughter! That's my daughter!" and an elated Rasha yelled back "That's my niece! That's my niece!" pointing at the only girl playing with a hijab. A row below, Pham Trong Linh hugged his wife and eagerly joined the

Roberto Porta-Córdoba

black teenager and his family in chanting the Brogdon last name over and over

The Destiny HS team didn't disappoint their fans and ended up winning the match with a categorical 25-15 victory in the last set. They had consumed the miraculous comeback and their fans were delirious. For the first time in school history, the Destiny HS girls were crowned state champs.

After the game, outside of the Destiny HS locker room, the proud parents, relatives, and faculty members hugged and celebrated with the girls. Several photographers from the league and local newspapers took pictures of the special moment. One of them suggested a picture of the entire team with their families. It was a hilariously difficult task, but in the end, the sports section of the state newspapers published the panoramic view photo of the young champions squatted in front of an Arab group of people being hugged by some Hispanic folks, next to a Black family embraced with an Asian one, in turn embraced with group of white fellows with tattoos, Verdi beards, and piercings. They all looked very different, some were giving a V sign, and others a thumbs up, but every single one of them had a beaming smile on their face. They all looked happy. They all looked pleased. They all looked possible.

173

Roberto Porta-Córdoba

Still D. B. Cooper

Most people in the United States spend Thanksgiving having dinner with their family or friends. Some spend it hijacking planes.

On Thanksgiving eve, November 24, 1971, a man in his mid-40s hijacked a plane flying from Portland to Seattle. The man, carrying a bomb, demanded $200,000 in ransom money and two parachutes, in addition to a fuel truck in standby at Seattle's airport. The airline met the demands, and after two hours of circling around, the plane landed and the 35 passengers were allowed to disembark without incident. During refueling, the hijacker instructed the captain to fly to Mexico City and gave him detailed technical directions about the flight plan, revealing in-depth knowledge of the aircraft and thorough planning abilities.

What happened next remains "the only unsolved case of air piracy in commercial aviation history." Just a few minutes after takeoff, the man parachuted out of the slow flying plane through the aft airstair, never to be seen again, taking with him the ransom money and the imagination of people for decades to come. News of the daredevil feat ran for days on all newspapers, radios, and television newscast of the time, and has been kept relevant by the countless investigations, reports, books, documentaries, and even movies made about it. Although millions of people had heard the story, Raffiel Braswell was not one of them.

175

He never knew about the hijacking, and thus was never intrigued by the whereabouts of D. B. Cooper, the pseudonym used by the mysterious hijacker. All that changed one afternoon.

It all started with an email Braswell noticed while deleting unwanted messages from his inbox. The message caught his eye because the subject said "SFC Malachiah Braswell-The Owl", his late dad's military rank and nickname, a nickname known only to close friends and family. The sender's name read "Troy E. Letang" and the email consisted of a polite introduction, some kind words about SFC Braswell, and a request to talk over the phone. Most importantly, the email said that the sender's father had served in the Army with the late Braswell. The area code didn't look familiar, but the sender said he lived in Rhode Island.

After showing the email to his wife and forwarding it to both of his daughters, Braswell searched online for the sender's name and was surprised as to how quickly he was able to track him down to Coventry, a small town in Rhode Island. Amazed, he also searched for his own name and couldn't believe how much basic information, even if not all up to date, he was able to find in a single Google search. Just like his daughters kept telling him, if he wanted privacy in the XXI century, he'd have to try another planet. Feeling he had validated Troy E. Letang's identity enough, and stung with curiosity, Braswell called the number the following day. A woman answered the phone and Braswell told her

Roberto Porta-Córdoba

about the email he'd received. The number turned out to be a landline telephone and the woman nicely asked him to wait while she went to look for her husband. When Letang got on the phone, he introduced himself and profusely thanked Braswell for his call. He sounded like a nice man. A long conversation ensued.

Letang told Braswell how his fathers had fostered a good friendship during their service as U.S. Army paratroopers, and how they had kept in touch despite taking different career paths, Letang's father as an airline pilot and Braswell's as a metallurgic engineer. As if they were old acquaintances, the two men chatted about their families, their jobs, their past, and the immediate future. None of them was too young to pass on a good conversation. Braswell was in his late 60s and nearing retirement. Letang was 65 and had just retired. Strangely, they sounded as close friends and felt comfortable sharing basic information about themselves and their families. The conversation turned out to be very pleasant.

-My father was saddened by your dad's passing –Letang said-. That was almost 10 years ago, right?

-9 years, to be precise –Braswell answered-. He lived a good life. He died in his bed.

-Just like my old man –Letang added-. He died in a hospital, but in his sleep.

-How long ago? – asked Braswell.

Letang paused. A sigh was audible through the phone.

-Last month –he said-. One week after his 90th birthday… and that's the reason…

He paused again.

-The reason for what? –asked Braswell.

-The reason for my email to you –replied Letang.

Braswell realized that they had talked about different things, but not yet about the seemingly important motive of the message he'd received.

-Yes, sir. I was about to ask you about that email –he chuckled-. I have to say that I'm intrigued. I didn't know if I should take it as a scam, a prank, or a sales pitch, you know?

Letang chuckled, too.

-I understand –he said-. Sorry for causing you trouble. I really appreciate you contacting me. All the phone numbers I tried were either disconnected or belonged to someone else.

After an epilogue about how technology had eroded whatever little was left of privacy these days, and its effect on social relations, Braswell felt it was time to cut to the chase and politely asked Letang why he wanted to talk to him.

In a tired voice, Letang went on to tell Braswell that his father had left a will, which included a request to contact the heir to Sergeant First Class Braswell, "The Owl", whose last address he had pinpointed to Raleigh, North Carolina. Letang brought up how his father had regretted not seeing more of him before health started to abandon both of them.

178

-The last time my dad saw your father was in 1989, during a paratroopers' reunion in Wisconsin. That's about 20 years before your father passed away – said Letang-. There are several pictures of them together. After that, they spoke many times over the phone, but never met again.

Letang added that the will stated to give Braswell's heirs an envelope with photos of their time in the military, a couple of old medals, some memorabilia, and a small-size package. However, the will specified to deliver these items in person, not by mail.

-Unfortunately, I cannot travel anymore –said Letang-. I have a bad back and I'm in permanent therapy, otherwise I would've loved to deliver these things to you. I've never been to North Carolina.

-That's all good –Braswell chuckled-. I don't live in Raleigh anymore. We moved to California years ago.

-Even worst! –Letang said, laughing and then coughing-. My back couldn't stand a 5-hour flight. Please forgive me.

-That's all good –repeated Braswell-. Let me see what I can do. I'm sure we can arrange something.

The men said goodbye after Letang wrote down Braswell's phone number and agreed to speak again shortly. In total, they had been chatting for half an hour. Braswell's wife found it a little odd given her husband's reserved personality, but it was obvious he

179

had enjoyed talking about his father and remembering him.

One entire week passed before Braswell could put his thoughts in order. He simply didn't know how to take this business about the will. It was an unusual request. Did the will really require those things to be handed in person? What was wrong with shipping them? It didn't make sense. Why would the late Mr. Letang include that detail on his will? Could it be just an eccentricity made up by his son? The only reason Braswell felt compelled to pay any attention to the whole deal was because the items Letang mentioned had a connection to his father. Otherwise, he might have told him to keep them. He told his wife and called his daughters to ask them their opinion. They were very dear to him, so dear that when they started their families and made him a grandfather, he convinced his wife to move to California to be closer to his grandchildren. One of the daughters lived in Santa Barbara and the other one in San Jose.

Braswell made the decision. He would travel across the country to pick up the memorabilia. One of his daughters would accompany him. Braswell's eldest grandson was graduating from high school the following year and the family had been planning to check some colleges on the east coast. It would work out perfectly. Braswell phoned Letang to propose some dates for the visit. Letang was very happy and apologized again for not being able to deliver the things himself or at least meet at a halfway point. After

Roberto Porta-Córdoba

another pleasant chitchat, Braswell was about to hang up the phone when Letang mentioned another oddity.

-Have you ever heard of D.B. Cooper? –he asked.

-Who? – Braswell said.

-D.B. Cooper, the man who hijacked a Boeing 727 in 1971 and jumped out with the ransom money? – Letang said.

Braswell paused for a moment and tried to recall.

-Not really –he answered.

-It's alright. Never mind –Letang said-. It's just an interesting true story. You may want to check it out. You can find it everywhere, in any computer.

Braswell didn't know what to say. He thanked Letang for the suggestion, reminded him to wait for an email with the confirmed dates of his visit, and said goodbye. "Who the heck was D.B. Cooper?" he was left wondering.

Two weeks later, Braswell sent an email to Letang with his arrival date to Rhode Island. It would be a month later, during spring break, to coincide with his grandson's college visits in the area. Letang was ecstatic and announced a fancy dinner at home for his visitors. Braswell thanked him and promised to take a fine bottle of California wine, although he wrote that he didn't want to create any burden for him. Braswell said he'd be happy just by receiving and seeing his father's memorabilia. "Nonsense," replied Letang, "you guys are flying a long way and we want to treat

181

you like royalty. That's what my dad would've wanted." The email would've been innocuous if it weren't for the last line Letang wrote. It read "Have you had a chance to read about D.B. Cooper?"

Braswell became curious. Who was this Cooper person Letang kept referring to? Why was Letang so intent on him learning about Cooper? Suddenly, Braswell began to have doubts. Was he doing the right thing by going to the house of a complete stranger... with his daughter and his grandson? Letang sounded like a good old man, and the story about both of his fathers checked out, but... what if he was a little cuckoo? He started to feel uneasy about the whole thing. His wife had already expressed some concerns, too.

His eldest daughter came up with a solution. She proposed telling Letang that they preferred to meet and have dinner at a local restaurant under the guise of not wanting to inconvenience him and his wife at home. Letang could bring the memorabilia package in his car and simply hand it over during dinner. Braswell liked the idea and wrote to Letang the following day. He feared that Letang might be offended, but in the end Braswell felt he had to find a balance between pleasing a recently made acquaintance and ensuring the safety of his family.

Although Letang was disappointed and insisted in having them for dinner at home, he accepted the proposal on the condition that the dinner be his treat. He didn't sound upset about it, but once again he

182

Roberto Porta-Córdoba

ended his email with the question "Have you had a chance to read about D.B. Cooper?" And this time he added: "You should."

Pleased with Letang's acceptance of his change of plans, and feeling more at ease, Braswell decided to find out who that frigging D.B. Cooper was. That same evening he sat down in front of his computer and began googling the exact name written by Letang. He immediately was swamped with hundreds of entries from Wikipedia, the FBI website, the Encyclopedia Brittanica, the New York Times, the History Channel, and hundreds of articles on websites as different and varied as HBO, Rolling Stone, Forbes, and Reuters, including some as unconnected as Major League Baseball, not to mention hundreds and hundreds of YouTube videos, so many that he kept scrolling down its search page for several minutes without end in sight. He found a staggering number of Cooper-based products in Amazon and eBay, ranging from books, posters, t-shirts, and LP records, as well as movies and documentaries from dozens of sources. In total, the D.B. Cooper search in Google returned almost 82 million results. Braswell was aghast. When he closed his laptop, two full hours later, his head was spinning, his eyes were dried up, and he almost stumbled walking to the kitchen.

His wife wasn't happy. She told her husband that Letang gave her a bad vibe. She thought Letang was a weirdo. Braswell asked her daughters if they'd ever heard about D.B. Cooper and both said they

183

hadn't, however, the youngest daughter's husband and the grandson who was to accompany him to Rhode Island recognized the name. The son-in-law said he remembered reading an article about the 40th anniversary of the hijacking years ago, and the boy said he'd watched a couples of the documentaries about him in YouTube and on TV. "What does this man have to do with anything?" wondered Braswell. "What's going on with Letang?"

As the date for the trip neared, Braswell and his grandson began to read more and more about the D.B. Cooper case. Whatever time he had free, Braswell watched videos and read articles about the peculiar hijacker. So did the boy. Half-serious, half-jokingly, they would phone each other to share their views and angles about the mysterious man. That's how Braswell learned not only about the meticulously planned hijacking, but also the specifics of the astonishing escape by parachuting from the plane. He learned about Cooper's precise instructions to the pilot not to exceed the speed of 115 mph without stalling the aircraft, and not to gain an altitude higher than 10,000 foot, while locking the wing flaps at 15 degrees, and keeping the cabin unpressurized.

Braswell and his grandson also learned how five Air Force fighter aircraft were deployed to follow the 727, but failed to make visual or radar contact with anything exiting the plane; and how it became impossible to establish a precise search area because of the cloudy dark night and the many parachute

184

maneuver variables in Cooper's control after jumping out of the aircraft. Braswell and the boy coincided how bizarre it must have been for the Reno airport authorities –where the plane ultimately landed- to see the 727 touch down the airstrip with the aft airstair still hanging and causing a huge tide of sparks as it scraped the tarmac. They also marveled at the fact that despite massive searches spreading over several years, over hundreds of square miles, and which accounted for thousands of combined resources from the police, Army, Air Force, National Guard, FBI agents, rangers, guards, private investigators, treasure hunters, self-appointed sleuths, exploration companies, and even a submarine used in a suspected lake, no significant material evidence was uncovered related to the hijacking. D.B. Cooper continued to be a fugitive for 45 years, until the FBI finally suspended active investigation in 2016. By the time Braswell began packing for the trip, he knew as much about the hijacker as the average Cooper fan. He was hooked.

The night before taking the short connecting flight to San Francisco International Airport, where he would join his daughter and grandson to continue the long trip across the country, Braswell made a phone call to Letang. He didn't need to do it -he'd already confirmed all the visit details by email- but couldn't resist telling him that he'd read a lot about D.B. Cooper and wanted to ask him why he'd suggested he did. In the last few days, after learning so much about the case, he had a hunch that Letang knew something that connected both of his fathers to the unidentified hijacker. At the beginning, he'd even speculated that his own father, Sargent Braswell, "The Owl," might have been D.B. Cooper due to his vast knowledge of aircraft and extensive training in military parachuting. However, when he saw the FBI sketch of the suspect, that possibility went out of the window. His father was black, D.B. Cooper was white. Then, could it be that the late Mr. Letang was D.B. Cooper? That would explain Letang's insistence in him learning about the hijacking case. But, if so, what connection would that have with his father? At the end, Braswell made the call, confirmed his arrival, and told Letang he'd got clued up about Cooper, but didn't dare to ask him the reason for his suggestion over the phone. "That's very good," was the only comment Letang made.

On the long flight east, with a stopover in Newark, Braswell and his grandson continued exchanging information about the D.B. Cooper case and trivializing about the many conspiracy theories and the dozens of self-declared suspects that had come forward through the years. The encounter took place two days later, not at a dinner, as originally planned, but during lunch, and not a local restaurant, but at the hotel restaurant. Ultimately, Braswell didn't feel totally comfortable meeting a stranger with his family at a place in a town he didn't know. He made up an excuse and politely asked Letang for his understanding. The old man obliged, only that he showed up alone, without his wife. He excused her

Roberto Porta-Córdoba

saying that she didn't have time to switch an appointment she already had at noon.

The meeting went well. Braswell introduced his daughter and his grandson to Letang and the four sat down at a secluded round table in a cozy corner of the restaurant. Letang seemed as jovial as he sounded over the phone, but he looked very fragile and emaciated. His white mustache, rescinding thin hair, and sunken eyes certainly made him look older than 65. Braswell apologized for the last minute change, Letang chuckled it off, but insisted that the lunch would still be his treat.

After several introductory topics of conversation, which included the grandson's college visits, and other courteous subtleties, the conversation finally turned to their fathers' friendship and the fulfilment of the late Letang's will. The man took out a manila envelope and handed it to Braswell. He couldn't help smile while seeing several photographs of his young father in military uniform and in paratrooper gear. Letang pointed and identified his own father, as well as other soldiers and airmen in the pictures. He seemed moved. The daughter and the grandson also looked at the photos with curiosity. Next, Letang took out a couple of rectangular velvet boxes and handed them to Braswell. They contained two honor medals and some Armed Services patches. Letang explained how much his father treasured them and that they had been earned by the team that included both SFC Letang and Braswell. He finally handed several folded cutouts from old military

187

publications that featured their squad and platoon. Braswell beamed with pride. He'd seen some memorabilia from his father, but none as old and revealing as this. He thanked Letang with a vigorous handshake.

-I will give you the package after dessert –said Letang, smiling.

-Oh, yeah –Braswell answered-. You mentioned a small-size package. What's in it?

Letang paused. His sheepish eyes glittered for a second.

-You'll see. You'll all see –he replied-. I left in the car. I just didn't want to bring it in here.

Braswell collected the envelopes, medals, and memorabilia, and put them aside on an empty chair. Suddenly, the known feeling of apprehension returned to him.

-That's all good –he said-. You can give me the package in the parking lot, but can I ask you a question?

-Sure –Letang answered with a nod, before sipping water from his glass.

-What's the deal with me reading about the infamous D.B. Cooper? Why were you so interested in me learning about that guy and the whole hijacking thing? –Braswell asked.

Letang seemed to have been waiting for the question. He settled in his chair.

-It is quite a story, isn't it? One that has been around for almost 50 years, now! I'm glad you read

Roberto Porta-Córdoba

about it. Did you also read about it? – Letang said, looking at the daughter and grandson with a grin on his face.

Braswell thought the man was really a cuckoo. A harmless man, but a cuckoo. Maybe his wife was right. His daughter and his grandson nodded yes to the old man's question.

Letang embarked on the story they already knew. How D.B. Cooper was never found and the whole aftermath after his hijacking. He added niceties that had escaped Braswell, but not his grandson.

-Did you know that there were 31 hijacking in the U.S the year after Cooper's? Did you know that half of these copycats also asked for parachutes? Did you know that all Boeing 727 aircraft had to be fitted with a device dubbed the "Cooper vane" to keep the aft airstair from lowering during flight? Did you know that Cooper's hijacking forced peepholes to be installed in all cockpit doors? This guy changed the whole industry –Letang repeated with excitement-besides fooling the FBI!

Braswell listened in silence. His grandson nodded in approval. The daughter grinned in surprise, not knowing what to make of Letang's witty outburst. After a few minutes, the old man paused his dissertation and Braswell broke in.

-But, sir, what does D.B. Cooper have to do my father… or your father? –he asked with a serious face.

Letang's face lit up. He settled in his chair again.

189

-More than you think –he replied with a wide smile-. More than you think.

Braswell went straight to the point.

-I know my father couldn't have been D.B. Cooper, but could he be *your* father? –he asked-. Don't tell me your old man was the one who pulled that off!

Letang's smile turned to a condescending smirk.

-No, Mr. Braswell –he answered-. D.B. Cooper was not my father and neither was yours. D.B. Cooper was older than them and was their Master Sergeant during their time in the Army. He was very close to them.

For the next ten minutes that felt like seconds to their avid ears, they listened to Letang, whose tone now sounded calmer and more deliberate.

-D.B. Cooper was not even D.B. Cooper – the old man began-. He wrote "Dan Cooper" on the plane ticket he bought in Portland, but some reporter misread it as D.B. Cooper and that's how it stayed the rest of the investigation. His real name was John Borden, and after he left the Air Force he became a commercial airline pilot, just like my father. He worked for NWA for several years, but felt disenchanted when he was passed over for promotion. He took his case to upper management, but his complaints fell in deaf ears. One day he decided to get even at the airline, he planned the hijacking and recruited our fathers.

Braswell was gaping. His daughter frowned slightly with skepticism. The grandson kept nodding with anticipation. Letang continued.

-Borden never told them exactly what he was going to do. He made them believe that he was part of an undercover government operation that included jumping out of a plane and required someone to pick him up at a drop zone. He told them that each of them could collect $25,000 for locating him in the wilderness. That is the equivalent to $160,000 in today's money! –Letang exclaimed-. My father told me that your father hesitated at the beginning, especially when Borden told them the operation would roll out on Thanksgiving evening, but since both of them had great appreciation for his former superior and felt a lingering loyalty to him, they accepted the job.

-Yes! I remember that Thanksgiving! – Braswell chimed in, nodding emphatically-. I was in 8th grade. My mom was furious because dad had to leave for work earlier in the week.

-That's right, sir –continued Letang-. I was about the same age and I also remember my dad not being with us at Thanksgiving dinner. Now we know why. Borden was a zealous planner. He chose three areas where he could likely land after the jump. He assigned one to my dad and another to your father. He calculated the third drop zone between the other two. Neither of our fathers knew Borden was skydiving in a business suit, with a fake bomb in a briefcase, and $200,000 wrapped around his waist.

191

Fictions of an Immigrant

-And where did he land? –the daughter asked, still with skepticism.

-He happened to land in your grandfather's assigned zone –Letang said, looking at her in the eye-. Let me show you.

The old man slowly unfolded a medium-size map that seemed to have been cropped out a larger one and photocopied many times. The map showed the region encompassing the states of Washington and Oregon. It had three ovals drawn with blue ink. Letang pointed at one.

-This is where Borden landed –he said looking at Braswell's daughter-. The west bank of Vancouver Lake, 16 miles north of Portland. Luckily that's a shallow lake and he didn't have to swim much. Your grandfather picked him up in a place now called Frenchman's Regional Park.

-But, how did my father find him in the dark? – asked Braswell, with a puzzled face.

-Well, he was "The Owl", wasn't he? By radio, sir. Borden had wrapped two military walkie-talkies in plastic and had fastened one on each leg. He recognized the lake and knew that your father would be in the west direction, around the park –Letang said, keeping his finger on the map-. My father was patrolling about 8 miles north, near a place called Campbell Lake. The three agreed on a radio frequency and memorized several codes to give each other's location after landing.

192

-That's dope! -the grandson said-. What would've happened if Borden hadn't made contact with neither of them? How would they know where to pick him up?

-Good question, son –Letang said, smiling-. My father told me that in that case, Borden was to walk to a specific marker on Interstate 5, where is now the town of Hazel Dell, and hide there until being picked up. Luckily for him, his jump was precise enough not to land too far off any of the three targets, despite the rain and the wind. The man was a beast. Not only a daredevil, but a hell of a skydiver.

Braswell and his daughter looked at each other. They didn't know whether to believe Letang or dismiss it as an embellishment of one of the countless conjectures found in the internet. They were speechless. Either Letang's father had helped D.B. Cooper for real, or Letang was the biggest liar and fraudster they'd ever come across.

-What about the money a kid found on the Columbia River years later? –Braswell asked, looking closer at the map-. Where is that?

-Oh, yes, yes –Letang replied, pointing at the photocopy-. He found them in 1980, right here, about 7 miles north of the spot your father met Borden. My father told me that the wind made Borden lose a couple of bill packets right after he jumped. I think it was about $6,000. They were already useless when the kid pulled them out of the riverbank.

-And what happened with Borden? –Braswell's grandson asked-. Is he still alive?

Letang smiled and sipped a little water.

-No, son –he answered-. He died of natural causes about 15 years later. He went back to work the Monday after the hijack. Can you believe that? My father said Borden chose the Thanksgiving long weekend precisely to conceal his absence from work. He requested the days off months in advance. The man continued to work normally for about two more years to avoid raising suspicions. Meanwhile, he started to exchange his money abroad, in his flying routes south of the border. Keep in mind the FBI had microfilmed each of the bills. Borden was over 60 years old when he passed. He died in Belize, you know. It was the perfect place to live a quiet retirement. Do you know where Belize is, son?

-Not really –said the young man- a bit embarrassed. His mother didn't seem to know, either.

-It's in Central America –broke in Braswell, with a chuckle-. South of Mexico. Right, Mr. Letang?

-Oh, yes, yes –he replied-. That is right.

-We're lucky you want to major in computers, not geography- said Braswell with a laugh, while patting his grandson on the back.

-Did you know that there have been dozens of thesis written about D.B. Cooper by creative writing majors to fulfill their master degree requirements? – said Letang, chuckling.

194

Roberto Porta-Córdoba

Letang slowly folded back the map and put it back in his pocket. He looked weary. Braswell felt it was time to wrap up the lunch and asked for the check. Letang insisted the lunch was his treat and for a few seconds jokingly wrestled the check with Braswell. Eventually, he let Braswell pay it, not without thanking him profusely.

-I still have to give you the package –Letang said, as they escorted him to the parking lot-

-That's right! –Braswell said-. I almost forgot. Where did you park?

Letang led them outside. He walked rather slowly. As they crossed the hotel lobby, Braswell's daughter asked him more questions.

-If Borden worked for the same airline he hijacked, how come the pilots or the crew didn't recognize him? –she said.

-I asked my dad the same question –chuckled Letang-. Borden was bald, but he used a toupee through the whole feat, and besides, he was stationed in Alaska and he only flew the Asian connecting routes. He only started flying domestically months after the hijack.

-And what about fingerprints? –the daughter asked-. My dad says he smoked like crazy while the plane circled around before landing in Seattle.

-No fingerprints –said Letang, grinning-. Borden was wary of them. So much that when a stewardess used the last match to lit a cigarette for him and attempted to throw away the empty card folder,

Fictions of an Immigrant

Borden quickly took it away from her and put it in his pocket. He was canny and methodical. He took everything with him!

The group made it to a 4-door sedan parked next to a fence in a guest spot. The questions kept coming.

-Did you father get to exchange his money, like Borden did? –the grandson asked, oblivious to the admonishing glance his grandfather shot at him.

-Oh, yes, yes! –Letang answered, as he opened up the car's trunk with his remote-. Remember he was also a commercial pilot, for a different airline, but flew the Caribbean routes all of the time.

-Is that the package? –Braswell asked, pointing at a medium-size bundle in the trunk.

Letang stood in silence for a moment, looking inside the trunk. His strange smile didn't match the sunken eyes and the paleness of his face. His facial expression exuded relief.

-Yes, it is –he said, as he dug it out of the trunk.

The package was carefully wrapped in shrink wrap. So well wrapped that Letang had to use his pocketknife to carefully cut a hole out of it.

-Don't tell me it's a helmet –anticipated Braswell, as the daughter and grandson looked on with curiosity.

Suddenly, he made out what it was. His eyes opened wide. For a few seconds he held the package in silence, as if trying to decipher what it meant.

Roberto Porta-Córdoba

-Oh, my Lord! –cried out the daughter, before muffling her mouth with her hand.

-Those are... bills! –the grandson said, gaping in disbelief.

Letang took the bundle off Braswell's hands and put it back in the trunk.

-It's your father's share –said the old man-. He never accepted it.

Braswell looked at Letang with bewilderment. He didn't understand anything. Letang looked over his shoulder before continuing.

-As soon as Borden uncovered to him what the "operation" had really been about, your father declined to take his share. My father told me he remained on task, supportive, and respectful until the three made it to the chosen safe house. But nothing, not even Borden's commanding presence or his soothing verbiage made him change his mind about rejecting his share of the ransom. Nothing.

The grandson asked if he could looked at the bundle a bit closer.

-What for? –his mother asked, still clapping her hand over her mouth.

Letang assented with a nod. The young man stuck his head in the trunk and keyed on his phone several of the bill's serial numbers clearly visible though the uncovered first layer of plastic. Braswell remained in total silence, looking at the bundle.

Fictions of an Immigrant

-Holy cow... –the grandson said softly with a shocked look on his face-. They're for real... they're for real.

He had entered the random serial numbers online in a website where the public could easily check if an old $20 bill was part of the loot from Cooper's hijacking. The three numbers came back as matched.

-Where's your vehicle? –Letang asked Braswell-. I'll move my car closer. You don't want to walk around with that small treasure.

Braswell remained quiet, now with his arms akimbo, looking at the bundle. Letang started to close the car's trunk.

-Wait! –Braswell said-. I'll carry it.

Letang froze. He gazed at Braswell with surprise.

-Careful –Letang said-. You got a fortune here. You can't safely spend these bills anymore, but you can sell them to collectors in the black market. The boy who found those $20 bills sold two of them at an auction for $6,500 each in 2008. You got 1,250 of those same bills in this bundle... and these are in even better condition.

-That's $8,125,000 –the grandson said, using his phone's calculator. His eyes sparkled.

-You're right, son –Letang said, in a suddenly invigorated voice-. Your grandpa doesn't have $25,000 here. He really has over 8 million bucks. I already jeopardized them by leaving them in the car. I'll park closer.

198

Roberto Porta-Córdoba

Braswell didn't say anything. He lifted the trunk lid and grabbed the package. It looked smaller now without all the shrink wrap around it. Without removing the first layer of plastic, Braswell counted 12 packets of 100 hundred twenty-dollar bills and one packet of 50. His father's share was complete.

-Do as you wish –Letang said-. But at least hide it under your jacket.

Braswell did just that. And more. He tucked the package under his loose windbreaker and walked decisively toward some bushes on the hotel's side garden. He'd seen a gardener when they came out to the parking lot and found him operating a small wood chipper. His grandson followed him. Letang and the daughter stay behind.

-Where are you going? –Letang yelled.

Braswell approached the gardener from behind and said something to him, but he didn't turn around because he had his ear muffs and couldn't hear him. Before the grandson or the distracted gardener could react, Braswell threw the packets of bills into the shredding hopper and watched. A quick, beautifully arched cascade of pulverized paper and plastic spat out of the machine and formed a small heap on the grass. Totally clueless and startled, the gardener only managed to see Braswell remove his windbreaker and use it as dustpan for the greenish heap.

-What happened? –yelled his daughter as she approached.

Braswell had an unreadable expression on his face as he walked past her and back to where Letang was standing in total puzzlement.

-Are you OK? –Letang asked him as he saw him coming.

-All is good –said Braswell, showing him the heap of cash dust.

He then walked to a near sewer drain in the parking lot, squatted beside it, and let the dust heap slide off his windbreaker. His daughter and his grandson hugged each other. Letang watched Braswell in silence, frozen in disbelief. Back behind the bushes, the gardener shrugged his shoulders, put back his ear muffs, and went back to work.

When he finished, Braswell stood up, shook off his windbreaker, and looked at the sewer drain.

-Where is the package? What have you done? – Letang asked him, with bated breath.

Braswell put his windbreaker back on, smiled at Letang, and looked over at his daughter and his grandson.

-I don't know –he answered, while putting a hand on Letang's shoulder and leading him back to the car-. I just know it was the right thing to do.

Letang looked him in the eyes, still in disbelief, as if demanding an explanation. Braswell paused for one moment. His voice sounded crispy.

-I just think I'm too old to start engaging in clandestine auctions –he said, arching his eyebrows

Roberto Porta-Córdoba

and staring down at the pavement-. And my grandson is too young to start believing in life shortcuts.

Letang looked over his shoulder attempting to give the sewer drain a last gaze.

-Good mysteries deserve to remain unsolved – Braswell added-. I think D.B. Cooper's is one of them. Don't you think so, Mr. Letang?

Today, years after having suspended the investigation, the FBI local field offices still receive occasional phone calls or emails from people claiming to have new information about D. B. Cooper.

Braswell and his grandson still enjoy reading and commenting about them. Good mysteries deserve to remain unsolved, indeed.

202

About the Author

Roberto Porta-Córdoba was born in the small town of Masaya, Nicaragua, in 1963. After graduating from high school in 1981, he moved to South Florida to learn English and attempt college. Because of fulltime work and a lean budget, he could only afford one or two classes at night. His bachelor's degree in Business Management took him 12 years to complete.

The author worked in retail until 1996, when he discovered his passion for explaining things during his tenure as human resources manager. He switched careers and at the end of 1997 he received a master's degree in Education. He then moved to his native Nicaragua to gain some international work experience.

Although the author intended to stay in his country only for a 2-year period, he met his current wife there and put off his return to the U.S. for 16 years. During this time, the author worked in government and pursued a master's degree in Political Studies in Spain. Upon returning to Nicaragua, he worked as a public servant in the educational field, later as a director in several nonprofit youth-at-risk programs, and lastly as a principal at an international high school, traveling abroad extensively during all these years.

In 2015, he moved back to South Florida with his wife and four children, before settling in Northern Virginia to work as a teacher, tutor, and author. This is his third fiction book published, his first in English.

203